Now Jake's eyes were like lasers, watching her, daring her to ask.

"What?" Izzy almost whispered even though she knew the answer.

"Attraction, desire—the tingle in your veins when you want to kiss someone and you know it's mutual. When you can't keep your eyes off each other, when the lightest touch causes a cascade of yearning, when you look for any excuse to be close, when you want the other person so much it burns. That was us."

His words slid over her skin, left a layer of goose bumps and an insidious prickle of desire. Now yearning did cascade. It shivered through her, igniting a stream of memories of the pull of attraction that had drawn them together—had caused need and fulfillment and joy. Took her to a time when a simple glance had made her skin heat, when the brush of an arm had sent delicious flutters of sensation through her. A giddy, dizzy sense of promise and anticipation.

Without even meaning to, she'd edged closer to him, as awareness permeated the air with a siren lure of temptation. One kiss wouldn't matter...

Dear Reader,

This book was special to write as I truly enjoyed throwing two people with an explosive past relationship into a situation where they are forced into close proximity *and* have a baby to look after!

Both Isobel and Jake have trust issues and they are still furious and hurt from their split six years ago. It was tricky getting them from this place to an ending where they can believe in each other and a happy-ever-after, but luckily the power of love did prevail.

I hope you enjoy reading their journey!

Nina x

Baby on the Tycoon's Doorstep

Nina Milne

Recycling programs
for this product may
not exist in your area.

ISBN-13: 978-1-335-55629-5

Baby on the Tycoon's Doorstep

Copyright © 2020 by Nina Milne

All rights reserved. No part of this book may be used or reproduced in
any manner whatsoever without written permission except in the case of
brief quotations embodied in critical articles and reviews.

This is a work of fiction. Names, characters, places and incidents
are either the product of the author's imagination or are used fictitiously.
Any resemblance to actual persons, living or dead, businesses,
companies, events or locales is entirely coincidental.

This edition published by arrangement with Harlequin Books S.A.

For questions and comments about the quality of this book,
please contact us at CustomerService@Harlequin.com.

Harlequin Enterprises ULC
22 Adelaide St. West, 40th Floor
Toronto, Ontario M5H 4E3, Canada
www.Harlequin.com

Printed in U.S.A.

Nina Milne has always dreamed of writing for Harlequin Romance—ever since she played libraries with her mother's stacks of Harlequin romances as a child. On her way to this dream, Nina acquired an English degree, a hero of her own, three gorgeous children and—somehow!—an accountancy qualification. She lives in Brighton and has filled her house with stacks of books—her very own *real* library.

Books by Nina Milne

Harlequin Romance

A Crown by Christmas

Their Christmas Royal Wedding

The Derwent Family

Rafael's Contract Bride
The Earl's Snow-Kissed Proposal
Claimed by the Wealthy Magnate

Claiming His Secret Royal Heir
Marooned with the Millionaire
Conveniently Wed to the Prince
Hired Girlfriend, Pregnant Fiancée?
Whisked Away by Her Millionaire Boss

Visit the Author Profile page
at Harlequin.com for more titles.

To my family for putting up with me during the writing of this book!

Praise for
Nina Milne

PROLOGUE

Six years ago

ISOBEL TRIED TO determine which emotion was uppermost, incandescent rage or sheer gut-pounding, rib-squeezing hurt. She opted for the former because she would not succumb to the latter. The thought of breaking down in tears prickled her skin with aversion—she would not give Jake Cartwright the satisfaction.

Instead she watched as Jake paced the room, each stride an angry re-treading of the past hour's conversation, his whole body taut with frustration. Then she hurled words, each one laden with fury.

'How could you do this? And why the hell won't you just admit it?'

'I won't admit it because I didn't do it. How many more times can I tell you this?' He halted in front of her. 'I did not sleep with Anna.'

Each word was enunciated with exaggerated emphasis.

'Jeez, Jake. Repetition doesn't make the words true. You must think I'm an A-grade idiot. Fact: I caught Anna sneaking out of your house at one-fifteen in the morning. Fact: she confessed!'

The memory so vivid. Beautiful, blonde, perfect Anna. Supposedly 'just a friend' from Jake's university days. Anna with her long blonde hair and endless legs and her first-class degree in economics and her brand-new modelling contract. Difficult to know which to be more threatened by.

Long hair tousled, shoes in hand, a cat that's had the cream smile on her face. A smile that had dropped from her lips with almost incongruous speed when she'd seen Isobel approach. 'Isobel? What are you doing here? I... we thought you were at work.'

'My shift finished early. I thought I'd surprise Jake.' The words had fallen from her lips on automatic, her tone ridiculously polite, almost conversational as the full ramifications of the scene pounded her brain. The irony not lost on her. 'Turns out the surprise is on me.'

'Isobel. Listen to me.' Anna's voice was urgent now, those wide blue eyes full of concern. 'There's nothing for you to say.' She side-

stepped to get around the willowy model, frowned when Anna reached out and took her arm.

'Wait. Please. Let me explain. Before you see Jake. Please Isobel. Come with me. Hear my side first.' Isobel hesitated; part of her wanted to storm in and confront Jake, part of her recoiled at the idea of seeing him now, fresh from Anna, perhaps still tangled in the sheets... The whole thought shuddered her body with humiliation.

'OK.'

'Thank you.' Anna's grip tightened on her arm. 'We can't talk here. There's an all-night diner round the corner.'

The walk achieved in a dull silence punctuated by the click of Anna's high heels on the pavement; images tormented Isobel's brain as realisation struck. Jake slept with Anna. Jake slept with Anna. Anger began to bubble, anger at him and anger at herself. How could she have been such a fool? Why had she agreed to date him? She should have known this would happen. Jake was gorgeous and rich and fun; used to women falling at his feet, He dated whichever beautiful model or celebrity took his fancy. Now he'd slept with Anna. Jake slept with Anna.

She followed Anna into a small café, redo-

lent with the smell of cooked breakfasts, fried eggs, the whiff of chip fat...

'Sit here,' Anna instructed, placing her handbag on a table as she gestured to Isobel. 'I'll get coffee. Americano right?'

Isobel nodded; it seemed easier than a refusal. Not that she could drink anything purchased by Anna—she'd probably choke. A few minutes later the blonde woman returned, sat down facing Isobel and leant forward.

'You have to forgive Jake. You have to. This was a one-off. I know it is. It's you he cares for and I think I was just a final fling before he commits. To you. I know he will be regretting it and it was my fault—my idea. Jake and I are friends. Nothing more.' Anna put a hand on her arm. 'It meant nothing. To either of us.'

Isobel shook her head. 'But it means something to me.'

'Please. You have to forgive him.'

Isobel rose from the table. 'No Anna. I don't.'

And she still didn't.

After her conversation with Anna she had felt too raw to confront Jake, her insides scorched with sheer humiliation, her brain leaden with the awful knowledge of betrayal. Instead she'd sat, sleepless, by the window of her small rented room until dawn had touched the sky. Sat and thought and soon the mortification had been replaced by a welcome bright bitter light of fury. An anger that didn't allow even the vestige of forgiveness.

Not that Jake was asking for forgiveness—instead he had the gall to try and turn it on her. Was furious with Isobel for not yielding to his will, for refusing to enter his illusory world where he was innocent. Shades of her childhood. Her stepfather's repeated lies and denials, the excuses that spewed from his mouth, his assertion that it was actually his wife's fault that he had hit her, that he was sorry, that he loved her. And Tanya Brennan always ceded and accepted him back.

No way was Isobel following that pattern—any pattern followed by her mother. Folding her arms now she glared at Jake. 'I have evidence and a confession.'

'You also have my word. I didn't sleep with Anna.'

'Then why was she tiptoeing out of your house at one-fifteen in the morning?'

'I don't know.' Jake gusted a sigh. 'But I can tell you what I think. Anna knew I was out. She still has a key from years ago when she stayed here whilst I was away. I think she used my house last night to entertain a "friend".'

'Then why didn't she tell me that?'

'Because she is seeing a man she has to keep secret—either a politician or someone married—she won't say. When she saw you, my guess is she panicked in case you stormed in and found him.'

'Then why doesn't she tell me now?'

'Because it could compromise him.'

Isobel shook her head. 'You have to admit that sounds sketchy at best. Anyway, if you weren't here, where were you? Prove to me you were somewhere else.'

'I can't. I was out walking.'

'Walking?' She could hear the high-pitched rise of her voice. 'Surely you can come up with something better than that? Walking where?'

'It's the truth. I had a bit of a row with my father.' Isobel stilled. In the months she had known him, Jake had mentioned his father less than a handful of times. 'I decided to go for a drive and then I parked and just walked.'

'So how did Anna even know the house was empty?'

'She called and I told her I was out for the evening. It was risky but Anna has always thrived on risk.' Yet another reason why she and Jake were suited to each other, Isobel thought dully. 'I get it sounds sketchy but it is the truth.'

Isobel stared at him.

She closed her eyes, realising she wanted to believe him. Knew she couldn't. The image of Anna, the way she had walked down the drive, the smile on her face, the urgency of her words—how could she disregard that? Plus, Anna was in Jake's league, beautiful, intelligent, wealthy. She was his type. Isobel wasn't. Isobel had grown up on a barren, desolate estate and then been consigned to the care system; Isobel only had the money she earned herself as a waitress; Isobel had dropped out of school at sixteen. This whole idea of dating Jake had been a mistake of massive proportions and now she was paying for her error in spades, clubs and her own heart.

Now he stepped forward and for a moment, despite herself, she was struck anew by his sheer aura, tried to remind herself that the thick blond hair, the charismatic blue-grey eyes, the strength of feature was a simple genetic chance. 'You have to believe me.'

Wrong choice of words.

That was what her mother had said time and again.

'This time I won't take your stepdad back. You have to believe me.'

Her stepdad talking to her mother. *'I won't hurt you again. I love you. I've changed. You have to believe me.'*

As if the phrase had some sort of hypnotic, magical mesmerism. The power to dictate.

She shook her head. 'No,' she said. 'I don't have to believe you. Not when all the facts tell me the opposite.'

Anger and hurt etched his face. 'Do you truly believe that I would cheat on you and then deny it, lie to you to your face?'

'I don't think you set out to do it, Jake. I think you and Anna got carried away in the moment, you took a risk because you genuinely thought I wouldn't find out.'

'That is not what happened.'

Isobel clenched her hands into fists—she would not believe him simply because she wanted to. Wouldn't repeat her mother's pattern. 'It's over, Jake.'

'Is that really what you want?' His voice was harder now, edged with intensity. 'Because it's not what I want. But it's your call. You either trust me or you don't.'

Be strong. 'I can't trust you. Not after this. And you can't have a relationship without trust.'

'Then I guess it's goodbye.' His voice was pure ice now and she forced herself to turn and leave the room. Refused to acknowledge the ache in her heart, told herself this was for the best. She was better off on her own—she'd always known that.

CHAPTER ONE

Present day

JAKE CARTWRIGHT LEFT the crowded tube station and strode forward through the throng on the pavement. He felt the welcome breeze on his face after the cramped underground journey. Sure, he could afford the chauffeured cars that his father took everywhere—hell, Charles Cartwright had a fleet of limos on tap—and he knew his father despised the fact that his son chose to use public over private transport.

Not that Jake gave a flying fish about his father's opinion. Not any more. He'd spent way too many hours of childhood caring about his father. Wondering why his dad didn't want him, why he lived with his grandfather, only saw his dad once in a blue moon.

Then, when Jake was six and his grandfather died, a limo arrived and Jake was chauffeured to Charles' London mansion. Jake could still remember his searing grief, his burning hope that his dad would be there to comfort him. A hope that had flickered out instantly—Charles hadn't even been home to greet his son. That had been left to Petra, Charles' PA-cum-assistant. It had been a prelude of times to come—Jake had been left to his own devices, his material needs looked after by Petra and the various interchangeable girlfriends and hangers-on that made up his dad's entourage.

Every so often Charles would see him, usually in company, each meeting always edged with awkwardness. Eventually Jake had decided to accept his father's indifference and lock down the emotional turmoil, all the questions, hurt and anger caused. Decided to get on with his life.

But now that Jake held a stake in the Cartwright empire, Charles Cartwright's apathy had turned to antagonism and he seemed dead set on thwarting his son at every boardroom turn.

Jake's pace increased—he would not let his father continue to run the business into the ground with his policy of extracting as much money as possible to spend on his hedonistic lifestyle.

For a moment the image of his grandfather flashed across his brain. *'You are the Cartwright heir, Jake. Never forget it.'*

And he hadn't—his life's ambition was to lead the company into a glorious future. Soon enough he would—in ten days, to be precise. In ten days he would wrest control from his father.

His phone rang and he pulled it from his pocket, noted the identity of the caller—Helen McKenzie, manager of the flagship hotel, Cartwright of Mayfair.

'Jake?' Helen's voice spoke of relief. 'I've been trying to get hold of you.'

'Sorry. I must have lost signal on the tube.' Jake pressed the phone to his ear, striving to block out the noises of the city—the familiar rumble of double-decker buses, the hum of mobile phones, the stream of chatter, the pounding of shoes on the sun-flecked pavements. 'What's wrong?'

'Um… A baby was left at Reception a couple of hours ago.'

Jake frowned. 'Did a guest leave her baby by mistake?' And not noticed for two hours? Unlikely but possible.

'That's what we thought at first. But then—' Helen hesitated. 'When no one came to claim the baby, I gave her to Maria to look after.'

'Good call.' Maria was the hotel's housekeeper, a mother of four with a brood of grandchildren.

'And I was about to call the police. But then Maria found a letter in the carrycot.' Deep breath. 'Addressed to you.'

'Me?'

'Yes. We haven't opened it, but I figured it was best to talk to you.'

Another good call. 'How old is this baby?'

'Maria thinks she is about three, maybe four months.'

'OK. Don't do anything. I'm on my way.'

Jake dropped the phone back in his pocket and moved to the kerb to hail a cab, knowing that would get him to the hotel fastest. His mind raced, told him that, whatever was going on, at least the baby couldn't be his. This past year or so he'd been so caught up in work, in his mission to gain control, he'd had no down time at all. His work hard, play hard ethos had morphed to work hard and work harder.

He took a deep breath as he climbed into the black cab and continued to process the situation, wondering who the baby belonged to and what she had to do with Jake.

Half an hour later he alighted outside the hotel and walked through the revolving glass doors into the opulent marble foyer, rich with exotic greenery, enhanced by the gentle sounds of the water feature to one side and enlivened by the sculptures on display by various London artists. He headed straight for the lift and to Maria's domain. Although Maria didn't live in the hotel she did sometimes stay and a room was available to her at all times.

Jake knocked and then paused on the threshold for a moment when the executive housekeeper called, 'Come in.'

Maria was sitting in her rocking chair by the bed where the baby lay asleep, surrounded by pillows. Both tiny hands curled into fists resting by her head, a head covered in a fine down of wispy brown hair. His breath caught in his throat as he registered the sheer vulnerability of this tiny being who had been deposited in his hotel and he felt a sudden stab of empathy. Left abandoned, unwanted—just like Jake had been.

His father had left within hours of his birth, jaunted off on a nine-month cruise. As for his mother, she'd hung around for a couple of days and then gone on her way and Jake hadn't seen her until he was eighteen. More memories crowded in. His mother's face, streaked with tears as she'd explained, the words tumbling out as though she had stored them up for years. She'd desperately needed money—her younger brother had been dangerously ill, but with the chance of a life-saving operation in the States if they could raise the money. She'd started a charity appeal and Charles Cartwright had contacted her and made a deal: marry him, provide him with a child and leave for a new life in the States—he'd pay for the operation, the aftercare and make a generous settlement.

'I had to do it, Jake.' His mother had dried her eyes, gazed at him with desperate appeal in her blue eyes. *'I had no choice.'*

Irrelevant. What mattered now was *this* baby. Jake was a grown man now, a success—that tiny, vulnerable, abandoned Jake had survived. Thrived. Grown into an uber-successful man with an ideal lifestyle.

'Is she OK?' he asked.

Maria nodded. 'She seems to be fine, an adorable bonny little *bambino*. I have given her a bottle and she went straight to sleep. She was left with a bag full of milk and nappies and clean clothes and a careful list of instructions about her routine. And here is the letter.'

Jake sat down at the small wooden desk and opened the envelope carefully, saw the barely legible scrawl that covered the scrap of paper inside.

Dear Jake
I know this will come as a surprise after all these years but I know I can trust you.

Emily is my baby, and I love her very much, but right now I can't keep her safe.

Martin, her dad, is coming out of prison tomorrow. Please, please, don't let Martin anywhere near Emily.

I hope it's OK but I have asked Isobel to come and look after Emily. I know that may be awkward but I trust you both and it will only be for a few days.

Please tell Emily I love her and I will see her soon. I have packed her milk and her teddy and some nappies.

Isobel will explain everything—but please keep Emily safe for me.
Yours sincerely
Caro Ross

Jake stared down at the letter for a long moment as memories streamed back. Caro—Isobel's best friend.

Isobel.

Her image danced up from the cache of memories.

Isobel, with her dark brown hair and hazel eyes that seemed to shift and change colour with her mood. Isobel, his first—his only—disastrous foray into the world of 'real relationships'. Perhaps it had been the folly of youth that had persuaded him to let his guard down, let Isobel in, to allow himself to believe emotions were a good idea.

Well, he'd been proved spectacularly wrong. Emotions had sucked—big-time—and the real relationship had been exposed as based on dust and ashes. *Whoa*—there was no point in a walk down memory lane, not when he knew how the path ended. With him, alone and rejected, stricken with disbelief and hurt as he'd watched Isobel walk away. Just as his mother had, exactly as his father had. Judged and damned as not good enough. Again.

Enough.

At that moment the baby stirred, gave a small whimper and then subsided back into sleep. Emily was the important person here, not Jake and his feelings—feelings that he'd long since got over. Isobel was history, someone who had been a mere fragment of his life. A blip, a mistake never to be repeated, a lesson learnt.

Jake had always known how to move on from the past—and he'd moved on from Isobel. Caro said Isobel would explain everything; ergo he needed to talk to Isobel. That would not be a problem. At all.

Isobel pushed open the door to her room that she rented as part of a flat-share with a couple of other girls.

And breathe.

It had not been a good day. Usually she loved her job, enjoyed the variety and satisfaction of being an events planner. But today the bride whose wedding she was helping to organise had had an enormous row with her mother, followed by an emotional meltdown on Isobel's shoulder. All over the colour of the bridesmaids' dresses.

On that thought her phone rang and she picked up. 'Hello. Isobel Brennan.'

'Isobel?' For a moment she almost dropped the phone. 'It's Caro.'

'Caro. Is that really you?' Relief and happiness intermingled; she hadn't seen nor heard from Caro for three years, every effort to contact her best friend stonewalled.

'Yes. It's me. It is so good to hear your voice, Isobel, and I'm so sorry for not being in touch for so long. And I'm sorry that I'm calling now because I need a favour. A huge favour.'

'It's OK.' Isobel could hear the break in Caro's voice, the quiet desperation. 'You can ask me anything, Caro.'

'Martin and I had a baby. A little girl called Emily. She's three months old and I love her so much. She is the best thing that has ever happened to me.'

'That's amazing news.' Isobel's head spun at the realisation that Caro had become a mother.

'Yes. But…' Caro took a deep breath. 'I'm scared for her.' Now there was heightened anxiety in Caro's voice, her every word edged with tears. 'Martin has been in prison—he wasn't around for most of my pregnancy or for the birth. But he's coming out tomorrow—I found out he's being released early—I can't let him anywhere near Emily. So I was wondering if… if you would look after Emily for me.'

'Of course I will.' Isobel didn't even need to think about it. She and Caro went back so far, had seen each other through so many hard times, had survived the care system together. There was nothing she wouldn't do for Caro. 'I'll come and get her.'

'Too risky. Martin has some of his goons watching me. But I gave them the slip. I think. I hope. I took Emily and I've left her with Jake.'

'You've done what?' Isobel could hear the increased volume, the positive screech of decibels in the last syllable and forced herself to breathe deeply. 'Sorry. It just took me by surprise.'

'I figured there is no way Martin would work it out. I slipped into the hotel, left Emily there. It seemed like the safest thing to do. Martin doesn't even know that I know Jake;

he does know I would turn to you. Jake has security systems and security personnel and… and, well, he's Jake. I trust him to keep Martin away from Emily. And I trust you to take care of her.'

The desperate certainty in Caro's voice utterly undid her and Isobel closed her eyes, reminded herself that the most important consideration here was Caro and Emily's safety. 'I understand. But what about you? When Martin finds out…' Her voice trailed off. Under his seemingly sophisticated, handsome exterior Martin was a violent psychopathic bully— a replica of Isobel's stepfather. 'You'll be in danger.'

'I know, but I have a plan, somewhere I can go and stay whilst I work out what to do next. But Emily is safer away from me. Just for now. I'm going to get rid of this phone now; that way, if Martin does find me he won't be able to track Emily down. But I'll contact you in a few days, I promise.'

'But…'

'I will be OK. Please promise you'll look after Emily. That's what matters most.'

The plea was so heartfelt that Isobel could feel her own heart ache and she knew she had to assuage the panic and pain in Caro's voice. 'I promise.'

'Thank you, Isobel. With all my heart. And thank Jake as well.'

With that, Caro disconnected. Isobel started to pace the room, tried to get her jumbled thoughts in order—fear for Caro, dread at the prospect of seeing Jake again, wonder at the thought of seeing Emily, a fierce determination to keep her promise to Caro.

Focus.

There was nothing she could do for Caro except do as her friend had asked. Look after Emily. The downside with the steepest of gradients was the fact that Jake was part of the deal. The *idea* of seeing him shivered her whole body with reluctance—she had no wish to come face to face with a reminder of her own stupidity.

Isobel had been a fool to trust him in the first place—should have remembered a truth learnt the hard way in childhood.

Love was an illusory emotion that rendered you weak.

Yet Jake Cartwright had woven a web of deceit so enticing, so beautiful that she had been charmed inside and for a short, magical time she'd believed that maybe, just maybe, fairy tale endings could happen. She couldn't have been more wrong—Jake had turned out to be an untrustworthy snake, a cheat and a liar.

But right now she'd have to pull up her big girl pants and face up to the necessity of seeing Jake the snake again. For Caro's sake.

At that moment her phone buzzed; one look at the display and the still familiar digits crashed her memory banks.

Before she could bottle it, she answered, 'Isobel speaking.'

'It's Jake.' Despite the fact it wasn't a surprise, his voice sent her tummy into instant freefall and she rolled her eyes in irritation with herself.

'You beat me to it. I was about to call you.'

There was a silence 'So,' he said eventually, 'I didn't see this coming.'

'Me neither. I know it's awkward but Emily and Caro are more important than any personal feelings.' Oh, God—she could only hope he didn't now think she *had* any personal feelings for him. *Moving on...* 'Is Emily OK?'

'She's fine. The hotel housekeeper, a lovely lady with kids and grandchildren, is looking after her in one of our suites. There's a security detail on the door and I'm working in here as well.'

Relief at the arrangements assailed her, forced her to acknowledge that maybe Caro had been right to know Jake would keep Emily safe from harm.

'How's Caro?' he asked.

'It's a long story.'

'Then I'll wait until you get here. I can send a car to get you.'

'No!' Her refusal was instinctive—she had no wish to be beholden to Jake at all. 'It will be quicker by train. I'll leave as soon as I can.'

'We'll be here.'

Once she'd disconnected, she inhaled a deep breath. This was OK—she could do this. No big deal. Moving at speed she packed a bag, then quickly changed into clean blue jeans, a dark grey top and black denim jacket. Boots, a swipe of mascara and a swipe of lipstick to give her a little height and a smidge of confidence and she was good to go. As long as she ignored the swarm of butterflies that swooped and fluttered in her tummy.

Isobel zipped up her bag, took one last look at her reflection and headed for the door.

CHAPTER TWO

JAKE STARED AT his laptop and tried to focus on his work. In the end he gave up, just as his phone buzzed. Isobel.

'I'm here. In the lobby.'

'I'll be right down.'

By dint of an intense effort he kept his body relaxed as he rose and walked over to Maria, who was feeding Emily. 'Isobel is here,' he said. 'I'll bring her up and then you can head home. Thank you so much for this afternoon, Maria— you have been a lifesaver. I don't know one end of a baby from another.' And in truth he had little interest in learning—babies were not his thing. His few encounters with them had rendered him a little bit uneasy, out of his depth.

'It has been a pleasure. This little *bambino* is beautiful.'

Jake nodded and then headed to the door of the luxury penthouse suite he'd moved Maria and Emily into and entered the lift, annoyed to realise that he was… what? Nervous? Edgy? This was no big deal. Isobel had been a blip. A blip he had long since moved on from.

Two minutes later he entered the lobby and scanned the occupants, trying to ignore the accelerated beat of his heart. There she was. Dark brown hair shorter than he remembered, skimming her shoulders in a glossy sweep. Her stance was the same, graceful yet wary, poised for flight or fight.

As if sensing his gaze, she turned and emotions walloped him.

A flare of anger he'd thought long since extinguished, a visceral punch of desire, his skin sheened with heat and then plunged into goosebumps. His system in overload.

Whoa. Isobel was a blip, remember? His pride demanded he showed her there were no hard feelings—there were no feelings at all. Shouldn't be too hard—he was his father's son after all. Not showing feelings was a walk in the park. He knew exactly how to mould his emotions, squeeze them, constrict them into the shape he needed them to be.

But the key was control and not to let unwanted emotions blindside you. Instead you got rid of them, sloughed them away. His feelings for Isobel were long since dead and buried and he would give them no chance of resurrection. This was just an odd reaction, one that meant nothing.

He moved towards her, a smile on his lips. 'Isobel. It's good to see you.'

Her dark eyebrows rose. 'It is?'

OK. If that was the way she wanted to play it, fine. 'Of course.' He summoned his most charming smile. 'Unexpected but good. Why wouldn't it be?'

Her eyes narrowed and he wondered if she would take up the challenge here and now; God knew he had no wish to replay their final showdown, but if need be he would. The way she had treated him still rankled and for an instant he relived the plummet of incredulous disbelief when she'd accused him of infidelity. The burn of hurt that she'd judged him guilty, that her trust in him was so fragile that she'd believe him capable of sleeping with someone else. That was the type of behaviour his father excelled in and for Isobel to believe he could or would behave like that had been a sucker-punch; it had seared his very soul.

He felt the smile harden on his lips as he held her gaze.

'No reason,' she said. 'Or at least none worth discussing. Especially as my prime, my *only* concern is Emily.'

Ouch. And touché.

'Of course. I'll take you straight to her.' He gestured towards the lift. 'This way.'

He eyed the confines of the space—surely it couldn't have shrunk in the past five minutes? Then Isobel shifted slightly and a flicker of her perfume assailed him, the jasmine scent familiar in its poignancy and a prelude to yet more memories. His senses stirred—the tickle of her hair against his skin, the taste of her lips, the sheen of her skin under his fingers, the touch of her on him.

Hell.

Clearing his throat, he strove for normalcy. Reminded himself that he'd Moved On. Capital M, capital O. This was an aberration—after all, from a purely aesthetic point of view Isobel was beautiful and, like it or not, years before the attraction between them had zinged into instant flame.

'I put Maria and Emily in our topmost suite,' he explained, relieved when the lift arrived at their destination.

He exited and waited as she followed him down a thickly carpeted corridor and stopped outside a door, where he nodded to the security guard posted outside. 'Stefan, this is Isobel, Emily's mum's friend. She's here to look after Emily.'

'Pleased to meet you.' Isobel smiled as Jake

knocked on the door and then pushed it open. He stood back and watched as Isobel entered the enormous, luxuriously furnished room and halted, her gaze riveted to Emily, who was cradled in Maria's arms. The older woman crooned a lullaby and he heard Isobel's breath hitch in her throat as she came to a halt.

'Maria, this is Isobel.'

Maria smiled. 'Hello, Isobel. Your friend's baby is very beautiful and so good. She has had a bath and some milk and we are now having a little cuddle before she goes to bed and I have told her not to worry; all will be well.'

Isobel stepped forward and smiled at Maria. 'Thank you so much for looking after Emily—I know Caro will be very grateful. This isn't her fault. I promise she loves Emily very much.' She reached out and stroked Emily's head and Jake's heart gave a sudden strange lurch at the gentleness, the awe in her touch. 'May I?' she asked.

Maria beamed and rose to her feet, carefully handed Emily across and watched in approval at the ease of transfer, the evident ease of movement as Isobel balanced the baby in the crook of her arm.

'Hey, Emily.' Noiselessly, Jake stepped a little closer, saw the baby's brown eyes widen as she gave a small gummy smile.

'You know what you're doing,' Maria observed. 'Do you have children?'

Now his heart lurched in a completely different way and a small exhalation of dissent or denial escaped his lips. Cue another mental slap-down—what did it matter if Isobel had found someone else, had a family?

'No, I don't. But my boss has a little girl and I've spent a lot of time with her. So I sort of have an idea.'

'You will be fine. Your friend left detailed instructions and enough milk and nappies for another few days. I will leave the two of you to it. All you need to do is put her down in her cot and she should go straight to sleep.'

'Thank you,' Jake said. 'And thank you so much for today.'

'It was my pleasure. You are a good boy. I know you will sort it out.' Jake hoped she was right. 'And if I can help at all you must ask. It is no problem.' With that she headed for the door.

Once it clicked shut behind her Isobel gazed down at Emily, who gave a small yawn, her tiny mouth forming a little oval as she waved her hands in the air. 'Maria is right. I think she is sleepy.' She sighed. 'I almost want to keep her awake, give her a chance to get more used to me, but I guess that would be daft. Probably best if I get her to sleep.' Emily yawned again and Jake nodded.

'I thought you and Emily could sleep in here.' He led the way to a bedroom, themed in gold and red, lush with velvets and dominated by an enormous decadent bed. A travel cot had been set up in the corner of the room.

'Emily will feel like a princess sleeping in here. You didn't need to put us somewhere so swish. Any room would have done.' There was a stiffness in her voice and Jake knew why. Isobel had always had an almost irrational suspicion of his wealth, loathed the thought that anyone would think she was freeloading.

'This suite is easier to secure—it's harder to get access to and no other guests will see the security guard on the door.'

A small sigh but she nodded. 'That does make sense. And on Caro's behalf thank you for all this, Jake. It must have come as something of a shock.'

'It's not every day a baby is left at Reception.' *Or an old flame turns up.* 'Obviously we need to talk. Once Emily is asleep, I'll sort out a room service dinner and we can figure out what to do next.'

Once Jake had left Isobel closed her eyes and exhaled a sigh, trying to find some kind of inner Zen. Yeah, right. That was so not happening. From the second she'd set eyes on Jake a hot surge of anger and hurt had roiled inside her, made worse by the fact that she had no choice but to feel gratitude to him for the way he was protecting Emily. It was compounded by something else, a latent spark, a frisson of something she was loath to identify.

Whatever it was, she didn't want to feel it—didn't want to feel anything. She'd got over Jake and she was staying over him. Her focus should and would be Emily and she smiled down at the baby.

And now her heart lurched, turned, melted—went through some sort of transformation. As if an instantaneous bond formed, so tangible she could almost see it shimmer into existence and in that moment she knew she would protect Emily with her life if need be. Dramatic perhaps, but also an absolute knowledge. 'I won't let you down,' she promised. 'Or your mum. I'll keep you safe.' And if that meant accepting Jake's help, she'd do it.

Carefully cradling the sleepy baby, she approached the travel cot, laid her down and tucked the blanket round her. Gently she stroked Emily's downy head, watched as the eyelids came down, saw the impossibly long lashes descend and her heart twisted at the baby's complete trust in yet another new person in her life. She waited until she was sure the baby was fast asleep and then she tiptoed from the room.

Isobel braced herself and moved forward, saw Jake standing at the enormous floor-to-ceiling window that showcased a magnificent view over London.

As she watched him her heart thudded in her chest with the sudden realisation that they were alone—an event she would never have imagined in her wildest dreams. As if he sensed her presence, he turned and she gulped. Why, oh, why was he still so gorgeous? He looked—older. *Well, duh.* He'd filled out; the lankiness of youth had bulked into a body that seemed to be all lithe compact muscle. His blond hair was shorter than it had been, cut close to his head. Grey-blue eyes, rainy day sky with a hint of sun held nothing she could interpret. Her eyes dropped and snagged on the firmness of his mouth and she took a step backwards.

Enough.

Jake might be gorgeous but his handsome exterior was a shallow meaningless shell that housed the soul of the man who had betrayed her.

His lips turned up in a smile but his eyes were wary. 'Is Emily OK?'

'Fast asleep.' She kept the reply short now as he gestured to the table.

'The menu's there.' He gestured to the sleek glass coffee table edged with mahogany.

'Thank you.' She could hardly refuse to eat with him; after all, they were jointly responsible for Emily and they had to come up with a plan of action—one that minimised the need for contact. He could set up the security and she'd provide the hands-on care. Simple. She perused the menu and her stomach gave a low grumble of anticipation. 'This is incredible,' she said, professional appreciation overcoming personal antagonism.

'Thank you. It's a new menu—I've just taken on a new chef and she's brilliant, if I say so myself. The sample menu she cooked for me was sublime.'

She could well believe it as she chewed her lip and deliberated the choices, eventually deciding. 'I'll have the wild turbot, please.' Casting a sideways glance at him, she asked, 'What are you going to have?'

'The lamb.'

'I nearly went for that. Because of the cocoa beans.'

'We could always go halv—' He broke off and frowned.

A frown she knew she mirrored. Because

that was exactly what they'd used to do—pick different dishes and share them. She gave her head a small shake, shocked at how easily they'd fallen into an old habit. Enough. There was a need to be civil—Jake was after all providing Emily with a sanctuary—but there was no need to be friendly. The grim set of his lips implied that this was a conclusion Jake had also come to.

'I'll order,' he said brusquely.

As he did so she walked to the window, marvelled again at the immensity of the glass and the panoramic vista. She turned and studied the surroundings properly, the cool grey walls, the simple yet flowing original artwork—a swoop of charcoal lines that depicted the flight of a flock of birds—the bold fun floral coverings on the sofa and armchairs, the decadent red of the velvet curtains and the eclectic scatter of designer lamps and statues of famous literary personages who had stayed at the hotel over the years, this history echoed by the original cornicing and panelling.

The stunning blend of old and new, the immense proportions were all a reminder of Jake's wealth and status and Isobel felt the old familiar sense steal over her—the same uncomfortable knowledge she'd had as a child—that she was a misfit. The one with fear in her eyes and bruises on her arms, then the 'foster kid' and eventually the ultimate reject, consigned to a care home because no one else would have her.

But now it no longer mattered—Isobel had built her own life, a world where she did fit. Jake's wealth and status were irrelevant and she would not be intimidated by them.

'Would you like a drink?' he asked.

'A soft drink would be great.'

'Elderflower cordial?'

'Perfect. Thank you.' The words emerged both stilted and wary as they eyed each other.

He handed her a glass and sat down opposite her. 'I'd like to know what is going on,' he said. 'Caro said you'd explain. I assume you and she came up with this plan together. But what I don't understand is why you didn't tell me first. There was no need for Caro to simply dump Emily at Reception and leave.'

There was definite anger in his voice and Isobel could see his point. 'I didn't know Caro was going to do that. I didn't know anything about this plan until a few hours ago. I didn't even know Caro *had* a baby until a few hours ago.'

'Excuse me?' Jake stared at her and inhaled deeply. 'I'm not getting any of this.'

'What did Caro tell you?'

He reached into his jeans pocket and pulled out a folded piece of paper. 'See for yourself.'

Isobel accepted the letter, perused it and tried to put herself in her friend's shoes. 'I think Caro had to come up with a plan fast and she came up with this. She may have been worried that you wouldn't agree to have Emily, she may have decided it was too dangerous to try to contact you first... I don't know. I haven't seen or spoken to Caro in three years.'

His eyebrows rose in surprise. 'But you and Caro were like family.'

'We were,' Isobel said softly and now sadness and guilt intermeshed inside her. 'But then she met Martin. And everything changed. At first he seemed perfect for Caro, appeared to worship the ground she walked on. But then, slowly, he started to change.' The change had been so gradual, so insidious that Isobel had told herself she was being paranoid. 'He became more possessive, started to control what Caro wore, started to put her down. Then he persuaded her to quit her job so he could look after her. Isolated her. Then one day he hit her.'

Jake flinched and his eyes hardened. 'Go on,' he said.

'Caro forgave him, said she knew he wouldn't do it again, that he was under a lot of stress at work and she'd provoked him. That he was truly sorry.' Isobel twisted her hands together, remembered her own clutch of fear as Caro had spoken. 'I told her to leave him, told her that this was the start. But all I did was antagonise her. And him. The violence got worse but she wouldn't leave him. Soon she was making excuses not to meet me. Then she told me she couldn't see me any more.'

The scene replayed in her mind, Caro's soft voice. *I can't leave Martin—he'd never let me go. And I need him. I love him and he does love me. I know he is sorry whenever he hurts me. He and I will work it out, but he's right. It's better if it's just the two of us.* The fervency in her voice, the desperate need to believe tore Isobel's heart. Her mother had said the same.

'I can't leave...'

'Simon loves me...'

'He's going to change this time...'

'I know he's sorry...'

She'd wanted to weep, to pound her fists against the walls, to do something—anything to save her friend. But she hadn't been able to, just as she hadn't been able to save her mother. The taste of another failure, the realisation that she'd let someone else down was bitter in her mouth.

Now she looked at Jake. 'I haven't seen or

heard from her since. I tried. Texted, called, wrote… Maybe I should have tried harder.'

'There was nothing you could do. If someone doesn't want to see you, they don't want to see you. You can't force them to.' Isobel glanced at him, heard the harsh note of experience in his voice and wondered at it. He rose and started to pace the room, a frown grooved on his forehead, his lips set in a grim line. 'This changes things.'

'Why?' Foreboding touched Isobel.

'What you have told me, what Caro has gone through appals me. Truly. And if I can do anything to help her I will. But right now Emily is my priority. I haven't set eyes on Caro for over six years and you haven't spoken to her in three. How do you know she is going to come back?'

The idea shocked her. 'Of course she will come back. Emily is her daughter. She won't abandon her.'

'You don't know that.' She glanced at him, saw the grim set to his lips. 'You don't know her any more. Can we contact her? Do we even know where she is?'

Isobel shook her head. 'She's going to call me in a few days.'

He drummed his fingers on his thigh. 'I think we should call the police.'

'No.' Her reaction was straight from her gut, born of visceral fear. 'You can't do that.' Isobel forced herself to remain still, to project calm. 'If we call the police, they will call social services.'

'Maybe social services need to be involved—maybe they can help.'

Now panic spiralled and she reminded herself that Jake didn't know how the system worked, didn't even know that Isobel had been in care. Because she'd never told him. She hadn't wanted his pity, hadn't wanted to further highlight the stark contrasts between their different backgrounds. 'How do you work that out?'

'Martin could persuade Caro that he is a changed man; she could get Emily and go straight back to him. You said it yourself. She has forgiven him time and again.'

'She won't do that to Emily.' Her voice was low as she tried to inject optimism into it, but she knew it was misplaced; Isobel's mother had loved Isobel, but that love hadn't been strong enough to withstand her dependence on Simon, nor had it enabled her to protect Isobel.

'You can't know that and the most important thing is Emily's safety.' His voice was inexorable.

Safe. Isobel knew what it felt like to not

be safe; it was a knowledge wired into her very being, her bones, her soul and she never wanted Emily to have to feel that. Images crowded in on her. Herself as a small child, huddled under her bedclothes, sounds through the walls, raised voices, the thud of fist on flesh, her mother's cry. Isobel's hand stuffed in her mouth to keep silent, the taste of her own fear, the weight in her gut at her own cowardice, that stopped her from flying into the other room to claw and fight and kick to protect her mother. The knowledge of what would happen if she did, the thud of the fist in her stomach, the shove, the twist of the arm. The loom of her stepfather's face before her, flushed and mottled, the words in her face, spittle flying.

Her own terror, the knowledge that she was defenceless. Just as Emily was now.

A conflict of emotions battled inside her but she knew her priority. 'I swear to you that I would never hand Emily back if Martin is in the picture. But please let's give Caro a few days. If there is any chance that she and Emily can be safe together we owe her that. Owe them that.' There was silence as he continued to pace. 'Right now, Emily *is* safe. Here.'

'That we can agree on. I will keep a full security detail on the suite; we have surveillance cameras here and there's me. I won't let Martin

anywhere near Emily. That's a promise. I hope
he turns up. Trust me, I'll enjoy meeting him.'

His voice was hard and as she looked at him
she knew he meant every word. Her gaze lingered on the ripple of muscle in his arms, the
sheer bulk and strength of him and a funny little thrill shot straight through her and warmed
her veins.

Stop right there.

Yes, Jake was big and strong, but surely she
could accept that without this daft, *stupid* reaction.

'Then Emily can stay with us? No police?'

There was a long silence and she could see
the shadows chase themselves across his grey
eyes, wondered what dark thoughts streamed
through his mind. Then he nodded. 'OK. Let's
give Caro a chance. You're right—she does
deserve that.'

'Thank you.' Relief ran through her, along
with reluctant gratitude. Enough to make her
smile at him. 'Really.'

'That's OK. As long as we are clear that I
will change my mind if circumstance dictates.'

Before she could answer, a knock on the
door heralded the arrival of their food.

CHAPTER THREE

JAKE MOVED TO the door, relieved to have a little space to process their conversation. Anger at what Caro had gone through, an ache for Emily, so innocent of the turmoil around her and the difficulties to come. But uppermost swirled thoughts of Isobel, her fear so palpable, her hazel eyes shadowed with darkness. Followed by her smile when he'd agreed not to call the police; its radiance had touched him. Which was not good. He had no wish to be affected by Isobel at all.

Pulling open the door, he smiled at the waiter. 'Thank you, Rashid. I'll take it from here.'

'No problem, boss.'

Jake wheeled the trolley into the room and Isobel moved over to help set the table, transferring the aromatic dishes onto the sleek cherry wood dining table. Jake froze momentarily, pushing down the urge to tell her not to bother, to please just sit down. Because, dammit, she was way too close. Which was causing reactions of a different and equally unwelcome type. Her scent tickled his nostrils and when her arm brushed his, his lungs hitched as desire tugged in his gut. A glance at her face showed her hazel eyes widen in mirrored reaction.

Now he did speak. 'Sit down. I've got the rest of this.'

Once seated, she looked down at her plate, studied its contents and he did the same, hoped that if he focused on the food it would ground him—remind him what was really important here. He tasted a piece of lamb, watched as she cut off a morsel of fish and followed suit. 'Fabulous,' she said. 'My compliments to the chef.' Another mouthful and then she met his gaze. 'So I guess we should figure out the logistics of the next few days.' She glanced round the suite. 'I can look after Emily here. If I need to take her out for some fresh air or to the shops maybe Stefan can come with me? You can get on with your normal life.'

Was she for real? Jake stared at her. 'That's not the way it will work. I'm staying with Emily too. In person. Caro made me responsible for her safety—that's not something I'm willing to delegate.'

'But wouldn't you prefer to be working?'

'I'll juggle it. Move a few appointments. It's only for a few days.' And right now, in the prelude to the board meeting, there wasn't anything urgent that needed his attention. Nothing he couldn't delegate or manage via email or conference call. 'After all, what about *your* work?'

'I spoke to my boss on the way down here and she is completely fine with me taking the time off.'

'Then it looks like we will be looking after Emily together.' He topped up their glasses, watching as she took another mouthful, and he sensed that her mind was still working on a way out. 'And I don't think we should remain here.'

That got her attention. 'Why not?'

'It's possible Martin will persuade Caro to tell him where Emily is. So, much as I would like to take Martin on myself, I'd rather Emily is completely safe, especially if he has hired muscle at his disposal. It makes sense to take Emily somewhere Martin can't find us. I was thinking about the Cotswolds. Near Oxford.' He had lived and worked there for a while and knew the area well. 'It's beautiful there and I think it would be a lot better for Emily not to be cooped up in a hotel suite for days. What do you think? If he does turn up here, Stefan and his security team will deal with it.'

Isobel looked considerably more cheerful. 'That does make sense but, given that it is truly impossible for Martin to find Emily if we go somewhere new, I may as well take Emily on my own. Or, to be completely safe, Stefan could come with me.'

An irrational feeling of hurt prickled his skin—it seemed clear that Isobel truly couldn't stand breathing the same air as him. 'So if I said to you that Maria could look after Emily, would you agree?'

'That's different. You are fulfilling your responsibility to Caro by finding a safe house for Emily, by providing a security guard.'

'Maria would provide Emily with love and care.'

'I am not leaving Emily.'

'Neither am I.'

She glared at him, picked up her fork, put it down again. 'I get you feel a personal responsibility but…'

And now his hurt solidified into anger.

'How about you tell me exactly what the problem is? Because I thought this was about putting Emily first and doing what Caro has asked. I thought it was about a small vulnerable baby who we both want to help.'

Heat flushed her face. 'That is exactly what this is about. But if we can figure out a way to minimise spending time together, I'd appreciate that. I thought you would too.'

'It's been six years. We have both moved on.'

'Yes, we have. But that doesn't mean I want to spend time with a man who betrayed me. Even if it was six years ago. Even if I am grateful that you are helping Caro.'

'I don't want your gratitude and I did not betray you.' Frustration seethed inside him at her obdurate belief.

She let a huff out and raised her hand in the air. 'Six years on and you still can't admit it. Why the hell not?'

'Six years on, why can't *you* just believe that I didn't do it?' It was a question he'd asked and asked himself in the aftermath of their break-up. He did understand how damning the evidence had seemed but Isobel should have trusted him. Why couldn't she? In the end he'd decided it didn't matter.

After all, for years he'd never understood how his parents could behave as they had either. What mattered was accepting it and moving on. Same thing with Isobel. Accept it and move on. And learn from it. He'd been a fool to open himself up to hurt, the possibility of being abandoned *again*. By anyone. So never again.

'This is getting us nowhere,' she said finally. 'But you're right. This is about Emily. She is why we are here and I will do my best to look after her. But I'm pretty sure it will be bad for her to have us at each other's throats the whole time we are looking after her.'

'What would you suggest we do? I can't admit to something I didn't do to make you feel better.'

'It's not about making me feel better.' Her forehead creased into a small frown. 'It's about closure. I want you to tell the truth. I want to know why you did it.'

Again the question hit him. 'Do you really have not a single doubt in your mind that I am guilty?' Remembered hurt bubbled and seethed underneath the barriers he'd erected.

Her chin tilted upwards. 'Nope. The facts speak for themselves.'

For a long moment they glared at each other, her hazel eyes hard with exasperation, frustration and amber glints of anger. And...hurt. All emotions he suspected he was reflecting right back at her.

He tried one last time. 'I didn't do it, Isobel. I swear it.'

And now, for the first time, he saw just a

glimmer of doubt cross her face, the faintest crease of doubt imprint her forehead, and he knew what they had to do. 'Give me a chance to prove it.'

'I don't understand.'

'We both want to do what is best for Emily, to look after her and keep her safe. I suggest we focus on that, but also use this time for closure. Six years ago we were both too angry for that. Now we can look at it with cooler heads.'

'The only way I'll get closure is if you admit the truth.'

'I have admitted the truth. Maybe the only way you'll get closure is if you actually believe me.'

'So you want to spend the next few days convincing me you were innocent all those years ago.' Every word was dusted with scorn.

'Yup. That is exactly what I want to do.' This was a chance for vindication, a chance to challenge and figure out her lack of faith in him. 'What do you think?'

What did she think? Isobel looked down at her near empty plate, her mind in tumult. She realised the conversation had absorbed her so completely that she had barely noticed eating the food, apart from vaguely registering that it truly was sublime. For a moment she focused on the last few mouthfuls and savoured each one, the hint of wild garlic, the tang of the chervil, and tried to concentrate her mind.

Then she looked up from her plate and studied his quizzical expression. She knew that he'd thrown down a challenge, a gauntlet.

'Do you really have not a single doubt in your mind that I am guilty?'

The impact jarred—all the stifled doubts from the past crowded back, hustled and jostled. Had she been wrong? No! She'd had evidence and a confession. Jake had been guilty as charged.

Then why was he continuing to lie? Was this some sort of game to him, a power thing? A need to trick her, a way to pass the time. Perhaps he quite simply had to win. Well, fine. Pushing her plate away from her, she smiled at him slowly, accepting his challenge. 'Bring it on.' He could spin it any way he liked; if he hadn't been able to convince her six years ago, there was no way he could do so now. But a discussion, a cool-headed debate would bring complete closure.

'Excellent.' Jake leant back and smiled right back at her and, to her consternation, her tummy did a funny little flip and a sudden sense of caution reared its head. Ever since she'd got here, set eyes on him, her body had kept reacting to him, almost as if their raw, visceral attraction still smouldered. Time for her hormones to catch up with the plot—this was all about closure.

'I suggest we agree to some ground rules. First, Emily is our priority—we need to make sure she is safe and happy. Any arguments or discussions about the past are kept to times that she is asleep. When we are looking after her, we focus on Emily and are civil to each other.'

'Agreed. It's a deal.'

It was far from the deal she had intended to make. Yet closure was a good idea. So why did she feel as if she'd made a deal with the devil?

Jake opened his eyes, aware that a completely unfamiliar noise had awoken him. It took his sleep befuddled mind a couple of seconds to orientate himself. Then he clocked the sound. It was a baby crying. Emily.

Instinct propelled him out of bed and into a pair of jeans. Shoving his arms into a shirt, he pushed open the door and raced into the living area.

He came to a halt as he saw Isobel standing by the window cradling Emily in her arms, making soothing sounds. She looked up as she saw Jake, her expression calm, no sign of the panic that cascaded inside him.

'What shall I do?' he asked. 'Is she OK?'

'She's fine. Just hungry. I'm waiting for the formula milk to cool down. Caro's instructions said she usually wakes up needing a feed about two and, right like clockwork, here she is, up and ready. Aren't you, sweetheart?'

'You should have woken me up. I could have helped.'

'It's fine, I can manage—you go back to bed.'

He shook his head. 'I'm awake now. I'll give you a hand.' After all, he was the one who'd insisted on looking after Emily together.

'OK.' Isobel moved towards him and his breath caught in his chest. She looked beautiful—dark hair tousled, hazel eyes bright but still flecked with a hint of sleep and dressed in a pair of flannel pyjamas with a fluffy robe pulled over them. Her cheeks were flushed and for a fleeting second her gaze lingered on his bare chest. Then her eyes hardened and she gave her head a small shake, the gesture dispelling the moment.

Looking down at Emily, she stepped closer to him. 'Why don't you take Emily and I'll get her bottle?'

Take Emily.

Panic surged. There was no way on this earth he could be trusted with so fragile and vulnerable a being.

'Better if she stays with you. I'll get the milk.'

He moved over to the kitchenette and picked up the bottle, wondering how on earth to check it.

'Dribble a few drops onto your wrist and see if it's room temperature,' Isobel instructed.

He did as she said and then, satisfied it was right, he handed the bottle to her and watched as she sat down, positioned Emily carefully and started to feed her, the baby guzzling happily, her tiny hands on the bottle. The surreal domesticity of the scene filled him with awe. The tenderness in Isobel's stance, the curve of her body as she bent over Emily, the dapple of moonlight on her dark brown hair all combined to unravel a strange rush of emotion inside him.

Perhaps it was sadness at the knowledge that his mother had never sat with him like this—he wasn't sure that anyone had, had no idea who had looked after him in the first nine months of his life, before his grandfather had stepped in. Whoever it was, he was grateful.

Isobel looked up. 'You're a natural,' he said.

'Not really. I only know what I'm doing because of Natalie.'

'Your boss's daughter?' She nodded. 'So
tell me what you're doing now. Not still waitressing?' Six years before, when he'd met her,
Isobel had been working as a waitress in a
high-street pizza chain. The memory of their
first meeting was crystal-clear even now. He'd
been at a school reunion, their booking at a
different restaurant had gone awry and they'd
ended up at a pizza place. Fine by Jake, but less
appreciated by others in the group.

Isobel had placed a pizza in front of one
such person, Hugo Fairley, who Jake had despised even when he was a small boy. Hugo had
turned and snarled at her, 'I'm not eating this
pigswill.' He'd flung out his hand in emphasis
and upended a jug of water and he'd lost the
plot, stood up and stepped right into her face.

Jake could still remember Isobel's expression—a flash of fear as she'd instinctively
stepped back, but then she'd held her ground—
and in that moment a mix of admiration and
a desire to protect the slender brown-haired
waitress had surged within him. He'd risen
to his feet and moved between Hugo and the
woman.

Blinking away the memory, he focused on

Isobel in the here and now, waiting for her answer.

'No, I'm an events planner now and I love it. I'm part of a small company, a two-woman band, and we organise weddings, corporate parties... Any and all events, really.'

'How did you get into that?' Against his own will he could feel curiosity rise. He liked the lilt of enthusiasm in her voice, the way her face lit up, the spark in her hazel eyes.

'After you and I broke up, I moved from the pizza place to working in a hotel. Waitressing again, but then I moved across to the catering team and from there to the events desk. I worked there for a few years, helping organise weddings, corporate parties, conferences, all sorts. Then Clara, one of the brides who held her reception in the hotel, someone I'd got on with really well, approached me. She was setting up an events management company and wanted to offer me a job. I took it.'

'Good for you. It sounds like a brilliant opportunity.'

He knew she would have more than deserved that opportunity. He remembered Isobel's work ethic—she was loyal, committed and worked her socks off in pursuit of her main goal—security. She'd not said much about her family, simply that her parents were dead and she was on her own.

'It was. Clara really knows what she is doing. She'd been in events for years but once she got married she wanted to work out a way to juggle a job and being a mum. So she started her own business. That way she could bring Nat to work with her and I pitched in and helped. Natalie has been to meetings, weddings, corporate parties… You name it, Nat's done it.'

'Sounds a bit like my grandfather and me. He took me everywhere with him; my earliest memories are of all the Cartwright hotels.' As always when he remembered Joseph Cartwright, his emotions were conflicted. Joseph Cartwright, the man who had looked after him for the first six years of his life, the man Jake had loved and had believed loved him back. The man he had mourned, only to discover years later that love had nothing to do with it. Because his mother had explained to him exactly why Charles Cartwright had wanted an heir. Turned out Joseph Cartwright had issued an ultimatum to his son.

'Provide me with an heir or I'll disinherit you, cut you off without a penny.'

So Charles had supplied Jake and Joseph had taken him in, not because he loved him—

but because he wanted an heir to mould in his own image as his legacy. And that was why he'd taken Jake to work with him.

'I'd make dens in his office, if we visited the hotels I used to play in the kitchens and in the housekeeping rooms. The staff were all amazing to me. The kitchen staff used to sneak me food and the porters let me play on the trolleys and help them with the luggage.' Perhaps, though, the supreme irony was that it had worked—the seed Joseph had sown flourished and thrived, at first because Jake thought he owed it to his grandfather's memory, and then because Cartwright was in his blood.

'I didn't know that.'

There was so much he hadn't told Isobel back then; he had been too intent on a demonstration of strength, all his assets and none of his weaknesses. So he'd kept his family out of it—hadn't wanted her pity. Now he contented himself with, 'I had a lot of fun.'

'So do Clara and Nat. We all do. I've been really lucky—building up the business together has been incredibly positive.'

'Sounds more like a partnership.'

'I hope one day it will be—that one day I can buy my way in. That's my medium-term plan. Along with getting a house. As soon as I can get a deposit together, I'll buy a student house. That way, I can live in it but also let the other rooms out.'

'You'll cover your mortgage payments and you can still save towards the partnership.' It was a good, well thought out plan. Clearly Isobel was still as goal-oriented—as he was.

'Yes.' Then a shake of her head. 'Listen to me. Telling you all this—there is no need for you to be interested.'

'I am interested.'

She looked down at Emily, but not before he saw scepticism flash in her hazel eyes.

'Did I say something so unbelievable?'

'Well, yes, actually. Why would you be interested? The amounts I am talking about are chicken feed in your world. You think in millions where I think in thousands. Plus I am talking about a two-person partnership; you deal with a global empire, make decisions that affect hundreds of employees. Compared to that, my plans pale into tiny insignificance.'

'It doesn't work like that.' Now she made no attempt to mask the sceptical raise of an eyebrow and his frown deepened. 'The amounts of money at stake aren't relevant. It's about your individual hopes and dreams—that's what's important.'

'But when you deal with the bigger global

picture, surely individuals all blur a bit, become like ants.'

'Nope. Because people are the most important thing, people are what make global empires tick. I've seen that.' Her hazel eyes studied his expression, her face animated in the low lights of the room as she listened. 'I spent four years working my way through all the different roles in the hotel industry.'

Her turn to frown. 'I thought your plan, your dream was to get a management role at Cartwright.'

'It was.' It was what he'd worked towards his whole life, the moment when he could start to make a difference, begin his quest to take Cartwright into the glorious future. 'Unfortunately, my father had other ideas. I went to see him, requested an undergraduate trainee post and he turned me down flat.'

Though he still didn't get why. To that date his father's attention to his activities had been negligible. Whatever Jake had asked for he'd acquiesced to without so much as a flicker of interest. But that time...

'Don't be daft, boy,' he'd said. *'What do you want to get involved for? Go and have fun. Party, live it up. Buy a yacht. Or two.'*

'I can have fun and work,' Jake had said.

Swallowing the obvious additional words. *Unlike you.*

His father turned up to board meetings when absolutely necessary, and otherwise spent his whole life in pursuit of pleasure, accompanied by an interchangeable array of trophy girlfriends and a ragtag crew of various so-called friends and hangers-on.

'*No.*'

Jake had waited, but that had appeared to be the sum total of what his father was going to say. Charles had headed to the door, picking up a jacket on his way.

'*Forget it, Jake. I say no and I'm the boss.*'

Isobel's voice pulled him into the present. 'So you went and worked for a different hotel?'

'Yup. A small chain based in the Cotswolds, owned by an amazing bloke called Marcus Elderflower. He took me on but said the best way to understand the business was to work in every role. I spent four years doing exactly that. I was a waiter, a porter, dishwasher, chauffeur, parking attendant, maintenance man, housekeeper, maid. I learnt that people are the most important part of an enterprise, each and every individual one of them.'

'And what about now? You clearly work for Cartwright now.'

'Yes. Once I reached twenty-five I came into

my inheritance proper—an actual sharehold-ing in Cartwright. That gave me automatic entry to the board.' And there had been zip his father could do about it. Though the fuss he'd made, you'd think Jake was the devil him-self, not his only son. As always, thoughts of his relationship with his father brought a bit-ter taste with them.

'And being management hasn't changed your perspective?'

'No, I see people as individuals. Like Maria, like Stefan.'

'But they are also your employees, cogs in the Cartwright wheel. When you make big de-cisions you can't just think about Maria and Stefan's needs.'

'Sure. But I owe every Cartwright employee the right to be a cog in a functioning, lucrative wheel, with fair wages and job security. To do that I do have to see each individual cog.'

Now she smiled. '*Touché*. Excellent answer.'

Jake realised he'd missed this—the exhila-ration of conversation and debate with Isobel. Years before, it had been underlain with a fris-son of desire, the spark of debate leading to the spark of desire. The animation on her face, the glitter in her hazel eyes, the vibrancy of her voice had always heated his veins.

Hell and damnation.

It still did and suddenly the atmosphere ratcheted as they looked at each other and he sensed Isobel's thoughts had veered down the same bit of memory lane. The discussions and debates from years before that had ended in laughter, or mock pillow fights or him sweeping her into his arms.

Her face flushed in the dappled moonlight that flooded the room, and he saw the tell-tale sign of awareness as her eyes darkened to a coppery hue he remembered so well. Now his gut tightened in an intense twist of desire, a yearning so deep it shocked him, almost rocked him back in his chair.

Emily gave a sudden small whimper and the moment was broken. Isobel blinked, looked down at the sleeping Emily and the spell broke. 'I… I need to get her to her cot.' She almost leapt to her feet as Jake nodded until his neck almost popped.

'Good plan. I'll see you at breakfast.'

CHAPTER FOUR

Isobel opened her eyes to the sound of Emily's gurgle and checked the time. Six-thirty and Emily must be hungry again, though for now at least the baby seemed content to wave her fists in the air and chat to herself. Swiftly, Isobel climbed out of bed and tiptoed to the bathroom, taking a moment to marvel anew at its proportions. The white-veined marble was cool and soothing, the enormous shower area boasted a double rainwater shower and as for the bath tub—she suspected she could swim in it. Large white candles, huge fluffy towels and two wicker chairs with towelling cushions added a sense of decadence.

Quickly, she availed herself of the facilities and returned to the bedroom, leaned over the cot and smiled as Emily cooed up at her. A quick nappy change and she placed the baby gently down on the plush velvet bed that dominated the room. Emily kicked her legs, her eyes seemingly focused on the hand-painted tropical-themed wallpaper as Isobel changed into jeans and a dark grey T-shirt.

'OK, sweetheart. Let's go.' Isobel picked Emily up and headed towards the lounge, telling herself that strange moment in the early hours of the morning had been imaginary, nothing more, brought about by lack of sleep and the surreal situation.

She saw Jake sitting at the table, netbook open. Short blond hair, shower-damp, T-shirt that showed off the swell of muscle—her tummy lurched slightly.

For real, Iz?

Irritation sparked inside her at her body's reaction. Again. This had to stop. But her brain seemed powerless to intervene, to prevent her gaze from lingering on the sculpted shape of his arms, the masculine beauty of his forearms, the strength of his wrists.

He turned and smiled. 'Morning.'

'Morning.'

He rose and went to the fridge, got out the milk she'd prepared the night before and popped it into a bottle warmer.

'Where did that come from?'

'Maria brought it round, along with some toys, and Stefan brought a sling. Apparently, it truly is the best contraption ever invented for transporting a baby.'

'That's a brilliant idea, actually—it will mean Emily is always attached to one of us, so if Martin turns up he won't be able to snatch her. I'll make sure I thank Stefan.' She glanced around the luxurious living area, the sumptuous furniture and plush rugs sprinkled now with toys and a play mat. 'And Maria as well. That's lovely of them both.' It was and it occurred to Isobel that perhaps they had done it because they liked Jake. That when he had said he did see his employees as real individuals he had meant it. Had she been unfair to him the previous night?

He handed her the bottle and she glanced at him. 'Would you like to feed her?' she offered. His head shake was a little too quick and, like the previous night, she'd swear she saw a flash of panic cross his eyes. She wondered why he was so worried about holding Emily. Was he worried that he'd drop her, hurt her or was there something more to it?

'Nope. I'm good. I'll make coffee. Breakfast is on the way.'

A few minutes later there was a knock on the door and Isobel went to sit at the table with Emily whilst he went and wheeled the trolley in, quickly set the table and served her.

Isobel inhaled the scent of coffee with gratitude, regarding her heaped plate with approval. Scrambled eggs, hash browns and bacon.

Heaven!

Once Emily had finished, she burped her, dropped a kiss on her head and then carefully placed her on the play mat on the floor. Emily instantly kicked her legs with glee, her tiny fingers reaching up to touch the brightly coloured hanging items. She smiled down at the baby. 'She is a happy little soul,' she said. 'I'm not sure if this is the right thing to say or not, but thank God Martin did go to prison when he did. It must have made such a difference to Caro's pregnancy and it allowed Emily to have a happy first few months.'

Like her own had been. Her mother had told her the story. How happy they had been as a family, poor but full of dreams and ambitions. Then it had all gone wrong. Her father, desperate to earn money, had engaged in a get-rich-quick scheme, agreeing to transport some 'stuff' for a 'friend'. Turned out it had been contraband, he'd got caught in inter-gang rivalry and in the crossfire he'd died.

Soon after, her mum had met Simon and any chance of happiness was gone.

It would not be like that for Emily or Caro,

Isobel vowed. This time she would pull off a happy ending.

'Isobel?' She blinked, realising that Jake was looking at her with concern in his grey eyes. 'You OK?'

'Yes, I was just hoping it all works out for Emily—that she stays happy. She's so vulnerable and small and trusting.'

Jake's gaze rested on the baby for a moment and then flickered away and again she could see shadows in his eyes. 'I hope so too,' he said. 'Now, are you all packed? I thought we'd head off after breakfast.'

'Works for me.'

A few hours later, and 'Nearly there,' Jake said as he exited the motorway.

Isobel leant her head back and simply gazed at the scenery as it rolled past, savouring the winding country lanes, bordered by rolling fields and hills of every hue of verdant green and russet brown, splashed with bright yellow crops. Occasionally they passed through picturesque hamlets with honey-coloured cottages that seemed to come from a bygone era.

Jake turned onto a gravelled driveway and parked. 'Here we are.'

A small huff of appreciation escaped her lips. The cottage was like something out of a fairy tale, made of stone, with blue windows and a white front door, surrounded by a splash of vivid red poppies. As she climbed out of the car she inhaled the glorious fragrance of spring flowers that pervaded the air. 'It's magical,' she said.

'Let's go see inside.'

For a moment as he hefted their bags out of the boot and Isobel took Emily out of her car seat she realised that to any passer-by they would look like a young family on holiday. The idea was strange—the realisation that this facsimile of family life might well be the closest she got to the real thing. If she and Jake had stayed together, this could be for real, perhaps they would have had a baby, perhaps—

Enough.

Perhaps meant nothing, the game of what-if a dangerous one to play as it excluded reality. Yet it seemed to her that regret tinged the air.

She followed Jake up the flagged path, through the trimmed hedges to the front door, where he opened the key box with the required code, pulled out the key and opened the front door.

They toured the cottage together. The interior was bright and light and airy, with a well fitted pine-themed kitchen, a cosy lounge with comfortable furniture and a large sliding glass door that opened out onto a magnificent garden. Upstairs showed two double bedrooms with en suite bathrooms; one of the bedrooms had a travel cot already set up in it.

They both laughed when Emily kicked her legs enthusiastically. 'She's right,' Isobel said. 'Actually, it's time for her nap. Though she did sleep for a while in the car.' She thought for a moment. 'I'll try it and if she doesn't sleep I'll get her up.'

'How about I go and make us a cup of coffee—we can drink it in the garden? With or without Emily.'

'That sounds good.'

Fifteen minutes later she joined him, sitting next to him on the slatted wooden bench that overlooked the myriad flowers and trees.

'Is Emily OK?'

'Amazingly, she went out like the proverbial light.' She sipped her coffee and then shifted slightly. 'You need to tell me how much I owe you.' No way could she let Jake pay for all this. In truth, however beautiful it was, a part of her wished he'd chosen somewhere more utilitarian, less…romantic.

'For what?'

'For this place. Also we need to keep tabs on what we spend on food and stuff.'

'You don't owe me anything. I'm doing this for Caro and Emily.'

'I understand that but I would like to contribute—Caro asked us both for help with Emily. This is a partnership. I'd like it to be an equal one.'

'An equal partnership has nothing to do with money.'

'It has everything to do with money.'

'But you can't base equality on money—that's wrong. Surely you don't think you aren't my equal just because I have a bigger bank balance than you.'

'Of course not, but in a partnership money is important. That's why I'm buying into a partnership with Clara.'

'But it doesn't always work like that. People can bring different things to a partnership. Two people can go into a partnership because one has money and the other has talent or connections. Clara may ask you to be a partner and waive a capital contribution because she values you and doesn't want you to be lured away by the competition, or set up on your own in the future. Or maybe she would prefer to have a partner, someone to share the risk with.' He raised an eyebrow. 'Do I need to go on? It's not all about money.'

Isobel's eyes narrowed as she recognised the

validity of his words and yet... 'That sounds great in theory but if I let Clara gift me a partnership I would always feel like the junior partner, the one who hadn't contributed my fair share.'

'Is that how you felt about us? Did my money make you feel like the junior partner in our relationship, our partnership?'

The unexpectedness of the question threw her for a moment. 'Your money did bother me.' A lot.

'I gathered. That's why you never let me pay for anything or take you to any fancy restaurants. We could only go to places we could both afford. Because you wanted to pay your way and pull your weight and not freeload.'

She narrowed her eyes, trying to gauge his expression and saw a flash of remembered exasperation. 'Yes, I did. What's wrong with that? I'm sorry if I didn't want to play Cinderella to your Prince or the Beggar Maid to your King Cophetua.'

'Excuse me?'

Isobel turned to face him, meeting his gaze full on, and saw that his exasperation had hardened to anger, but she was damned if she would back down. 'You heard me. Paying my way mattered to me.'

'And I understood that and I respected it. I

had no wish to be your benefactor—I never saw you as Cinderella or a beggar girl. But at the end of the day I do have money and I'm damned if I'll apologise for wanting to spend some of it on taking my girlfriend to a posh restaurant. It's not a sin to be rich. That's part of who I am—suck it up.'

There was a silence and Isobel turned to look at him. 'Maybe we should have said all that six years ago.'

'Maybe we should have.'

She replayed his words and, almost against her will, she gave a small gurgle of laughter. Their gazes met, his eyes still dark with anger. 'Something funny?'

'Suck it up?' she asked.

Now his eyes softened and she saw the small tell-tale tug of his lips as he tried not to smile. Then, 'You're right. I shouldn't have said that. I should have said, Suck it up, Cinderella.'

Now they both began to laugh, and she could feel the tension dissipate and fly away on the spring breeze. Turning to him, her breath caught. He looked so—*gorgeous*, and he was a man who could laugh at himself, who could see the funny side of a fraught situation. The idea churned her up inside—it was suddenly hard to see this man as the villain of the piece. And yet she had to. Because the alternative was—what? Leaning over and brushing a kiss on his cheek? Accepting that he had been innocent six years before? Neither option was possible.

Jake looked at her. 'But clearly we should have talked about the money thing more. I had no idea it bothered you so much.'

'That's because you are the one with the millions in the bank. But try to imagine that you haven't, picture an empty bank account. Then along comes a woman with shedloads of money, and you start dating. She wants to eat in fancy restaurants where she foots the bill, buys you clothes so you can conform to the dress code, she buys you diamond cufflinks and designer clothes... How would you feel?'

'I'd feel uncomfortable.' Her eyebrows practically reached her hairline in mute challenge. 'OK. I'd hate it,' he admitted. '*But* if the relationship was worth it, I'd figure out a way round it.'

'Exactly. And I did. I figured the only way to make it work was if we only went to places I could afford, places where I would fit in.' She regretted the last words as soon as they left her lips, as his grey eyes turned to lasers.

'What do you mean, fit in?' he asked.

'I—it doesn't matter.'

'Yes, it does. Because this is what we agreed—

to talk, to aim for closure, to try and figure out what went wrong.'

Jake was right and if she wanted him to tell her the truth about Anna, then she needed to be truthful too. That way, maybe she'd get why he had strayed. Maybe her attitude to money had exasperated him more than she'd known—it made sense that he'd missed his usual lifestyle, the expensive venues.

'It wasn't only about the money side of it or being able to pay for my half of the bill. I didn't feel comfortable in fancy restaurants. I didn't know how to behave. I didn't fit in.' In truth, she had never felt she fitted in anywhere, still wouldn't feel comfortable in his milieu. 'I didn't have the right clothes. The right background.'

'None of that mattered. You could wear a bin bag and you would still behave with grace and politeness.'

His words touched her and she smiled at him; without thought, she reached out to touch his arm. The contact was electric and for a split second she froze in shock—the feel of his skin, the swell of his forearm under her fingers sent a sharp tingle through her body. She pulled her hand back in attempted nonchalance, looking away from him at the beauty of the landscaped garden, the riot of flowers, the neatly trimmed green of the hedges. Tried to refocus on the conversation.

'Thank you. That's kind, but it's not true. Everyone in those restaurants, everyone at the glamorous yacht parties you asked me to—they would all have known I didn't fit.' The very idea had made her soul shudder with horror. 'I didn't know what to say, how to act around the rich and famous, the glamorous—your crowd, in other words.'

'All you had to do was be you. You had nothing to be ashamed of or worried about.'

She could hear the bafflement in his voice. 'I wasn't ashamed. It felt as though you were slumming it with me and everyone knew it. All your previous relationships were with glamorous celebrities who meshed with your lifestyle. Your friends were all wealthy or university graduates with posh backgrounds.'

Bafflement morphed into concern and he turned on the bench, placing his coffee cup on the ground. 'Look at me. Whatever our differences, I swear to you I never once felt I was slumming it with you. Education and background don't define you. That would never make any difference to me.'

Isobel shook her head. 'But it made a difference to me. You had a private education, went to uni, could buy anything you wanted.

One day you will run a huge global empire. It made me feel…inadequate, a fish out of water. Maybe that's why it was so easy for you to sleep with Anna—she was your type, your natural fit, someone who would go to glamorous shindigs, would enjoy being seen at fashionable restaurants.'

'Anna was a friend, or at least I thought she was at the time. I didn't sleep with her. Why would I have, Iz? Because you're forgetting something important here, something we had. Something that had nothing to do with background or education.' Now his eyes were like lasers again, watching her, daring her to ask.

'What?' she almost whispered, even though she knew the answer.

'Attraction, desire—the tingle in your veins when you want to kiss someone and you know it's mutual. When you can't keep your eyes off each other, when the lightest touch—' and now he glanced down at his arm where she had touched him earlier '—causes a cascade of yearning, when you look for any excuse to be close, when you want the other person so much it burns. That was us.'

His words slid over her skin, leaving a layer of goosebumps and an insidious prickle of desire. Now yearning did cascade; it shivered through her, igniting a stream of memories of the pull of attraction that had drawn them together—had caused need and fulfilment and joy. It took her back to a time when a simple glance had made her skin heat, when the brush of an arm had sent delicious flutters of sensation through her—a giddy, dizzy sense of promise and anticipation.

Without even meaning to she'd edged closer to him as awareness permeated the air with a siren lure of temptation. One kiss wouldn't matter...

Then Emily's wail emerged from the baby monitor at her waist, shattering the spell. Isobel leapt to her feet, striving for composure. 'That's Emily,' she said unnecessarily. 'I'll go and get her. I think we should take her out this afternoon.' That way they could avoid a resumption of this conversation. They were skating perilously close to the edge of doubt, the chasm of attraction, both black holes she must not fall into.

He nodded. 'Agreed.' He gave her a glance and she wondered if he was as shaken as she was at how close they had come there. 'Why don't we go boating? In Oxford.'

'That sounds perfect.' They couldn't get up close and personal in a boat.

CHAPTER FIVE

AN HOUR LATER, with Emily safely strapped in her sling and securely attached to Isobel, they approached a brightly coloured red-striped gondola-shaped paddle boat, watching as it bobbed jauntily up and down on the water next to the jetty.

Jake climbed in first and then he reached out a hand to steady Isobel as she followed suit. Gingerly, she placed her hand in his and he told himself that a simply friendly gesture shouldn't impact him any more. But it did; the feel of her fingers in his was stupidly evocative, ridiculously provocative, and each fleeting touch seemed to add another drop of fuel to the slow burn of desire building up. Isobel had always had this effect on him, been able to conjure up desire with the most ephemeral of touches or the simple beauty of her expression. He'd assumed that reaction would be nullified by the bitterness of their break-up, by the elapse of time. Clearly not. Their spark was still smoking and he knew reigniting the flames would be disastrous—would distort and blur closure.

So he would block it, guard against the insidious tendrils that were trying to pull him back into a web he had no intention of entering. Isobel had rejected him, judged him and found him wanting. Game over with no chance of a replay.

Yet this time her accusation about Anna hadn't delivered the same sucker punch of anger and hurt as before. Because, for the first time, Jake could see the glimmer of a reason why Isobel *might* have found it so easy to believe. If she truly thought Anna was his type, if she'd spent months thinking she didn't fit into his life... So now he had to make her see that her reasoning was at fault. As the man who had persuaded most of the Cartwright board to his way of thinking, he could do this. He could make Isobel see the truth, in the same way he'd shown the board that his plan could and would work.

He blinked, seeing that Isobel had narrowed her eyes, suspicion etched on her expression. 'You're looking very pleased with yourself.'

'No reason not to be. The sun is shining, we're on this beautiful river, teeming with wildlife.' And indeed it was a timeless setting—sun motes dappled the blue-green of the water, the riverbank abounded in shades of green and a warm breeze carried the hum of insects.

He leant back and studied the pedals in the centre of the boat. 'Probably best if I pedal and you look after Emily.'

'Works for me.' She adjusted the sling so that the baby could see the ripple of the water. 'I think she likes movement and colour—she was fascinated by the wallpaper in the hotel suite.'

'She's got taste—that is hand-painted wall-paper.'

Jake started to pedal, enjoying the feel of the small blue boat cleaving the water, yet his eyes returned again and again to Isobel; she was relaxed, her dark brown hair ruffled by the breeze, a smile on her face as she chatted to Emily. He watched the way she looked at the baby, her focus absolute as she talked, pointed out the sky and the water, tickled her under the chin and elicited a small gurgling chuckle. The way she held her, the utter vibe of safety and caring and love she exuded—it filled him with awe.

'Oh, look.' Jake followed her line of vision and brought the boat to a halt as he spotted a brood of ducklings followed by their mother swimming into their path. 'Ducks, Emily. They go quack-quack.' The baby smiled a gummy smile and Jake couldn't help but smile as well.

'We may spot some swans as well, and keep an eye out for kingfishers. If we get close enough to the bank you should see dragonflies and there are lots of butterflies here as well.'

'You sound like you've done this a lot.'

'When I was working at Elderflower Hotels Marcus liked his staff to be able to talk knowledgeably about local activities so I came on a few boat trips for research. Then sometimes I'd come out because I like it—it's peaceful out here on the water.'

'Was it strange working for a different hotel?'

'It wasn't what I had planned to do but it was the best thing I could have done. Marcus was right—it's the best way to learn the business, a chance to appreciate how a hotel works and what makes it tick. It gave me the basis for a business plan—reward your staff. They make or break a hotel, so pay them fairly, include loyalty bonuses. I want Cartwright to be authentic, individual, environmentally aware, fun, an escape or a home away from home, something for all guests.' He stopped and rolled his eyes. 'Jeez, I sound like a politician addressing a rally. Sorry!'

'Don't apologise. It's a fantastic ethos.'

If only his father agreed. Jake's jaw hardened. In a week or so his father's agreement wouldn't be necessary, would be an irrelevance and Jake would have control. He felt a sudden qualm and he pushed it away. His vision for Cartwright was the right one—he knew it and he'd spent the past four years slowly convincing the other minority holders of it. But all attempts to persuade Charles Cartwright had been stonewalled. At the board meetings his father had sat, an unreadable expression on his face, and simply voted against any proposal Jake put forward. If asked for a reason he simply said, 'We want to maintain the status quo.' That was his vote—end of.

Jake assumed his father was worried the money would dry up, that his lifestyle would be at risk, that Jake wasn't capable of taking control. Each time frustration welled inside Jake, each vote against him the equivalent of another kick of rejection from the man who had fathered a son to avoid disinheritance and who'd handed that son over as a commodity.

But soon enough his father's wishes would be irrelevant. Next week the rest of the board would give Jake their formal support and his father would have no choice but to comply—because he would be outvoted.

Emily made a sudden noise, tugging him

from his reverie, and he watched as she kicked her chubby legs happily, her tiny hands reaching out as if she wanted to trail them in the water. Awe touched him at this tiny happy life—mixed again with a sadness that he had never engendered such feelings.

Isobel too was watching Emily, her expression soft as she stroked Emily's hair, and then she glanced at him. 'Do you think you'll do this for real some day? Come here, or somewhere like it, on a real family day out?'

'No.' Easy to give an unequivocal answer. 'I'm not interested in marriage or children. I've figured out a great work/relationship balance and a lifestyle that suits me down to the ground.'

'So how does that work?' Her voice was a tad over-casual.

'Right now, work is my priority so I haven't even dated for the past couple of years. And that suits me—a long-term relationship wouldn't be fair, even if I wanted one. Which I don't. When work calms down I will start dating again, but I like my relationships to be short and sweet.'

He couldn't help but note that the temperature in the boat had sunk to chilly.

'And how does *that* work?'

Jake kept pedalling, resisting the urge to let

a defensive note creep into his voice. He had no problem with how he handled relationships.

'I'm upfront with any woman I date that I'm not looking for anything serious. Just a few weeks of fun. For both of us.'

'So you take a woman out for dinner and over the caviar and champagne you explain you only want to see her for a few weeks but don't worry, it will be fun?'

'Yes. It's honest and upfront. If she's looking for more then we enjoy dinner and go our separate ways.'

'Define fun.'

'Depends on the woman.' The one thing he would never do was what his father excelled in—treating women like a generic set of trophies. His father used gifts to buy people; he had a closet full of jewellery, designer clothes, expensive watches that he'd use to woo his succession of trophy girlfriends. Or to apologise for his numerous infidelities. Jake had vowed never to be like that; any relationship he had would be tailor-made to the individual. 'Some women prefer to jet off for a skiing holiday, others prefer a more tropical location, some prefer seclusion, others prefer glamorous yacht parties.'

'So they tell you what they want and you buy it for them?' Her outrage was clear from her expression, though she was careful to keep her voice even and low so as not to upset Emily. 'It sounds like an all-expenses-paid holiday. With a bonus available if they perform well.'

Anger surfaced and he forced himself to keep the boat on an even keel, aware of Emily, who was happily engaged in trying to get her toes into her mouth, oblivious to the increasing heat of the exchange above her. 'If I take a woman on an all-expenses-paid holiday what is actually wrong with that?'

'Because you are buying them.'

'Some women are willing to be bought.' His voice was hard. Just as his own mother had been bought. 'But those aren't the type of women I'm interested in. I don't take them on holiday in return for their sexual favours. I date women I like and who like me back. We enjoy each other's company and we're both honest enough to say what we want. A non-messy, uncomplicated time together.'

'It just seems a bit shallow.'

Jake shrugged. 'Then shallow works for me. There's no chance of anyone getting hurt and it leaves me free to focus on work.' That was what drove him—the desire to take Cartwright into the future, make it larger, more global. He would not be like his father, simply living off his grandfather's spoils; he wanted to earn his living, deserve his wealth.

'So you see a relationship as a hindrance to your work.'

'Hindrance is a strong word. But I think it would be unfair to commit to a relationship where I would always put work first as a priority. That's why my work/relationship balance works for me.'

'You didn't see us as short and sweet.'

'No, I didn't.' His relationship strategy had been devised after Isobel. No one could say he didn't learn from his mistakes. With Isobel he hadn't planned, or calculated or thought. From the moment he'd intervened in the pizza place all he'd wanted was to be with her. It had been nothing like his previous relationships, all quick flings with celebrities or other wealthy socialites. Isobel had been different—he'd let his guard down, allowed himself to care, succumbed to the foolish possibility of love. And ended up hurt and disillusioned. Par for the course. Once he'd believed his grandfather loved him, only to discover that to the old man he had been a commodity, a prize, the coveted heir, a tool to further his own ambitions. When he'd gone to live with his father he'd longed for love so hard he could still feel the ache of remembered hope in his gut now.

All he'd met was indifference, not dislike, but he'd sensed he discomfited his father, made him almost squirm with discomfort. It had certainly not been love, though his father denied him no material thing.

The outlines of a pub appeared around the curve of the river and he pointed to it. 'How about we moor the boat and grab something to eat?' he suggested. And once there he would definitely change the subject.

Twenty minutes later they were seated in the outdoor garden of the riverside pub, Emily in a baby bouncer provided by the friendly waiting staff. A weeping willow draped its branches into the water and the lazy drone of the river life hummed in the air. The pretty rustic tables were scattered over the newly mown grass, the scent of which tinged the air.

A waiter brought their food to them—steak and kidney pie for Jake whilst Isobel had opted for the king prawn, crab and chorizo linguine. A tantalising aroma arose from both dishes and she gave a small murmur of appreciation.

That was until Jake looked across at her. 'So what about you?'

'What about me?' Isobel twirled some linguine carefully around her fork.

'Are you in a relationship?'

Isobel hesitated, gently touching the baby bouncer as she saw Emily's eyes starting to close. She realised she could hardly refuse to reciprocate in giving information. 'No.'

Was it her imagination or did some tension drop from his powerful shoulders; did his jaw seem to relax a smidge?

'Like you, I'm very focused on work and—' she shrugged '—I like being on my own. For now, at least. Maybe for ever. But definitely until I have security, a house of my own, money in the bank.' Free and clear of any sort of dependence on another, be it for money or happiness. 'Then—who knows?'

His expression was quizzical now. 'What if you meet someone now? You can hardly ask them to wait until you have security. Why not buy a house together?'

'Because that's not what I want to do. If I did that it wouldn't be my home and I'd have to—'

'Compromise? Share?'

'Yes. No…' She glared at him, realised how hard it was to explain. But Isobel knew she wanted to own her own house, needed it to be hers and hers alone. One of the worst things about foster care had been not having *anything* of her own. Having to live in bedrooms decorated by other people, bedrooms used by other foster kids. Knowing any minute she could be moved on without warning. No way would she risk having her home taken away from her. Having a joint mortgage, it reeked of being in someone else's power. 'It's too risky. If you buy a house with someone and you split up then where does that leave you?'

Now surprise flickered across his face. 'So you don't believe in the fairy tale ending or the happy ever after of marriage?'

'No.' This time there was no hesitation. 'Not enough to bet my house on it.' Isobel's mother's relationship with her stepfather had run the gamut of negativity—destructive, violent, rife with his infidelities and her mother's forgiveness of everything in the name of love. A love that created debilitating dependency and gave Simon power. Isobel would never be dependent on anyone, never cede power. Love made you weak; independence made you strong. Simple.

'You're saying you'd rather have ownership of bricks and mortar than a relationship.'

'Yup.' No question in her mind. 'Then, once I have that, have security, I'd consider a relationship. With an equal, with security of their own, who will enhance my life.' But not someone she needed. 'I'd prefer we lived separately, had our own lives as well.'

He hesitated and then said, 'He sounds a bit like a wind-up toy.'

'Excuse me? He sounds nice and kind and he'll be there for me...'

'Whenever you want him. Someone who you choose to bring out whenever you feel like it. Someone with a prescribed amount of money in his bank account, not too little and not too much. A customised wind-up toy.'

Isobel shrugged. 'Then a wind-up toy works for me,' she said. 'Just like shallow works for you.'

'And what about kids? How do they factor into this separate house, equal partnership?'

'They don't.' Isobel looked down at Emily and for a moment regret shivered through her, that she would never have a baby of her own.

Now his eyebrows jolted up in surprise. 'You don't want children?'

Again she wondered, as she had done so many times, if her decision was foolish. But then all her reasons resurfaced, the ones she had been over time and again since she'd split with Jake, and she shook her head. 'No, I don't.' The idea was too scary, the responsibility too much, the risk too great. For a moment she recalled an overheard conversation between two social workers, after yet another of her foster placements had broken down.

It's tragic, what her mother has done to her,

what the system has done. And at this rate the cycle will continue, like it always does.'

The words had stuck with her and, whilst she knew it wasn't always the case, statistics did show that patterns often repeated. What if she was a rubbish mother—what if she let her child down, the way her mother had let her down time and again? Or, come to that, the way she had let her own mother down. The thought made her feel clammy inside.

'No, I don't,' she said firmly. 'I love Natalie but I am happy to hand her back at the end of the day.'

The words were not wholly true and she could see the look of puzzlement on his face— could see more than that. His blue-grey eyes studied her for a long moment. 'I'm not buying it,' he said eventually. He gestured towards the sleeping Emily. 'I've seen you with Emily. You're a natural and you're amazing with her. I can see how caring you are and I can't believe you don't want a baby of your own.' Now his gaze met hers. 'Years ago I got the distinct impression you wanted them. We even discussed what our hypothetical children would look like.'

The conversation was still fresh in her memory, played itself out in her mind, so clear she almost felt she could reach out and touch their younger selves, hear words murmured as dawn had streaked its first light through the open bedroom window.

They'd been sitting up in bed, hand in hand, leg against leg, backs against the headboard, draped in the silken cotton of his expensive sheets—a moment of intimacy, of closeness, where words could be spoken without thought or censure.

She'd looked up at him, studied his eyes, the length of his eyelashes. 'If we have a baby I hope she gets your eyelashes.'

'And your eyes,' he'd said. 'And your hair and your smile and—'

'No! Definitely your hair.'

He'd turned then and something sad had flashed across his eyes. Then he'd shaken his head and reached out to her. 'And perhaps right now we should put in a little practice in how babies are made.'

'Hmm…they say practice makes perfect.'

And then conversation had been forgotten as they'd slid into each other's arms, the sense of desire familiar and yet achingly, intensely precious…

Isobel blinked the memory away, caught his gaze, saw his pupils darken and knew he'd re-played the same memory reel. 'We both said a lot of things back then,' she said flatly. 'Any

baby discussed was strictly hypothetical.' As
well as foolish—the idea of having Jake's baby
had been mooted when she'd been living an il-
lusion, not knowing that the curtain had been
about to fall, exposing the sham for reality.
After Jake she'd toughened up her stance on
relationships and children, relearnt the lessons
first absorbed in childhood. 'Anyway, what
about you? How do kids fit in with short and
sweet relationships?'

'They don't,' he said, echoing her own ca-
dence and phrase. 'They can't. It wouldn't
be fair to father a child if I'm not willing to
commit to its mother. And if I had a child I
wouldn't leave them.' His voice was filled with
determination and she recalled that his own
parents had split when he was young, that he'd
ended up with his father.

'But don't you want a child to leave the Cartwright empire to?'

It was clearly the wrong question; he physically flinched and his eyes were shadowed with
anger. 'That is not a reason to have a child.'
His voice was harsh and, as if he realised it,
he inhaled deeply, his voice calmer when he
resumed. 'Anyway, I may have a child who
loathes the hotel industry.' He looked across
at Emily again and she saw a sudden sadness
in his face as his gaze rested on the baby, her

eyes closed, her hands curled into tiny fists. Now curiosity touched her. Years before had he ended their hypothetical baby conversation because he knew even then he didn't want kids?

'Fair enough—then let me rephrase the question. Don't you think one day you may want to move on from "short and sweet"? You can't want to work all your life. So maybe one day you will want to settle down.'

'Nope. But even if, hypothetically speaking, I did change my mind—let's say I meet someone and we get together—there is no absolute guarantee that we would want to stay together. Odds are I wouldn't get custody and anyway I wouldn't want to take a child from his or her mother.'

'Then you share custody. You would still be your child's father—you would still play a huge part in your child's life. Lots of couples manage it.'

'And kudos to them. It's not something I could "manage"—especially if my ex decided to move abroad, or remarry.'

'But you may not break up.'

'There is a huge possibility. Think of the divorce statistics.'

'But—' She was sure there was a flaw in his argument—she just couldn't seem to spot it. Because he was right—there were no guarantees. Yet she *knew*, whatever Jake was telling himself, there was more to his decision to eschew parenthood.

He glanced at his watch. 'We'd better head back.' It was a clear signal that the conversation was over.

By the time they got back to the cottage Emily was more than ready for bed and Isobel decided to skip the baby's bath and get her straight down before she got over-tired. Emily was asleep almost before she had been lowered into her cot after her night-time bottle. Isobel tiptoed to the door and exited.

She paused on the threshold as she saw Jake standing in the kitchenette, studying the carton of formula milk powder, and watched as he carefully spooned formula into a bottle and then moved to the kettle and poured the water into the bottle.

Again her heart thudded with a strange sense of warmth—brought about by the intense look of concentration on his face that brought a smile to her own. A man who was such a success in the boardroom, a multimillionaire who whisked women off to tropical islands, doing something so domestic made her smile.

It brought a question to her lips. 'Out of interest, do you do domestic? I mean, do you hoover your house, clean your own bath?'

He looked up. 'Actually, yes, I do. I even have a duster.'

Was he telling the truth? His deadpan expression gave her no clue.

He screwed the teat back on the bottle and made an attempt to shake it to mix the powder in. A spray of milk emerged, straight onto his shirt and hair. He cursed and Isobel couldn't help it; she giggled. The slapstick moment on top of the idea of Jake wielding a duster was too much.

'Sorry,' she said. 'I truly didn't mean to laugh but—'

He glanced down at himself ruefully. 'It's OK.' And then he chuckled. 'I was trying to be helpful.'

'And I appreciate that. I really do.' And she did. 'I'll show you how to do it if you like? There's a technique. First time I tried it with Natalie's bottle I had a similar accident.'

'I'd like that.'

Isobel headed to the kitchenette, scooped powder into another bottle and handed it to Jake, waiting whilst he poured the water in from the kettle.

She took it from him and stepped closer to demonstrate. Too close—way too close.

Focus. But not on his body, the sculpted forearms, the swell of his upper arms, the strong thighs. Not on his smell, not on the way his hair spikes up—

This was a bad idea but, for the life of her, she couldn't figure a way out of it.

'Put your thumb over the top of the teat, so you're blocking the hole. Then you shake. Like this.'

Her voice emerged squeaky…breathless… *ridiculous.*

He'd moved even closer to her now and his eyes held a wicked glint that ripped the breath from her lungs.

'So it's all in the wrist action,' he said straight faced and her gaze flew to meet his, in shock at the double entendre.

'I—'

Then he grinned and wiggled his eyebrows. 'Sorry, I couldn't resist. Puerile but—'

'Yes,' she said, trying to keep a straight face. 'Definitely puerile.' But she succumbed to a giggle, which morphed into a full-blown laugh. And in seconds he had joined in.

Now their gazes locked and she could feel the shift in the atmosphere, the swirl of desire, the fugue of need. They were even closer now. His scent tantalised her, the warm smell of baby milk mixed with a hint of citrus-sharp shower gel and a whiff of bergamot. Her head whirled and there was an utter inevitability about what happened next. She wasn't sure afterwards who initiated it, who made the fatal decision or whether it was a completely synchronised movement.

But one step took them closer and then she was in his arms and her lips met his and oh, God, it felt so good. His lips were so familiar and yet so new, and her lips tingled as tremors of raw desire shuddered through her body. Gentle, hesitant at first as if they both feared rejection and then the kiss deepened, intensified, searing through her veins. His fingers tangled in her hair, she pressed her body against his, wanting more, her pulse rate accelerated at his taste, his scent, the way his kiss could drive her to the edge of desperate need for more. Her body was alight and craving more of him—of Jake—she wanted his touch, wanted the satisfaction her body knew and remembered.

Then an image of Anna penetrated the haze of desire, her cat-that-got-the-cream expression as she'd exited Jake's house. What the hell was she doing? She pulled away and they sprang apart, staring at each other for one appalled instant. How could she have been so stupid?

This was the man who had cheated on her, splintered her heart.

Humiliation roiled inside her, clashed with the still present desire and doused it. She swiped her hands across her lips and saw emotion shadow his eyes, a glimmer of hurt.

It didn't matter. Nothing mattered. Sheer mortification started a slow burn as she stumbled backwards, trying to process what she'd just done.

Fool!

An urge to run nearly overcame her but then she realised there was nowhere to run to; she was stuck here, in this perfect cottage, with the man she'd kissed as though her life depended on it.

Well, if she couldn't run she'd have to stand and face the music, accept that she had orchestrated it herself. 'I'm sorry. That shouldn't have happened.'

Jake's expression was neutral, completely unreadable as he leant back against the counter. Until she looked more closely, saw the clench of his jaw, the tautness of the folded arms.

'No. It shouldn't. But it did.' He dropped his arms to his sides. 'All we can do is make sure it doesn't happen again. Put it down to a moment of stupidity.'

'Utter stupidity.'

'Stupid, yes. Surprising, no.'

'How do you figure that? I am plenty surprised.'

'Really?' He held her gaze now and she felt heat creep up her cheekbones. 'We always had a spark, straight from the get-go, and I guess that's hardwired into us.'

'That spark was six years ago and was well and truly eradicated when you cheated on me!'

'Then explain what just happened. I wasn't the only person involved.'

She'd love to be able to claim exactly that, but she couldn't. 'That kiss was a throwback— an aberration.'

'Or your body knows something that your mind won't accept. It knows I didn't cheat on you. Knows I had no reason to.'

The intensity of his voice rocked her, her body and mind still caught up in that kiss, her whole being still seared with sensation and desire and need as she sought an answer.

He stepped towards her and then back again, his gaze never leaving hers. 'I have never felt this level of attraction to any other woman. There was no way on the planet I would have slept with anyone else.'

Now there was a longer silence. In the burning aftermath of that kiss his words rang with

truth; the knowledge of how completely physically attuned they had been strummed her
body. Isobel stared at him, heard nothing but
truth in his voice, saw only sincerity in his
eyes. And yet…anyone could lie. So many people had lied to her. Social workers who had
promised her that her mother would turn up
to see her, foster carers who had told her this
was her 'for ever place', told her they 'loved
her'. Words meant nothing, could be spun and
used. Sincere gazes could be practised in front
of the mirror.

And yet this time her gut told her that Jake
was not speaking falsely. Had she been wrong?
Or did she want to believe him? Perhaps the
physical attraction had messed with her head.
Instincts warred inside her—her gut rolled,
racked with indecision.

As her mind whirled it took a while to register the buzz of her mobile phone. She pulled it
out of her pocket, looked down at the familiar
number with relief and quickly accepted the
call. 'Hey, Clara.'

'Hi, Isobel. Can you talk for a minute?'

'Of course.'

CHAPTER SIX

JAKE WATCHED AS Isobel moved away from the kitchenette to the living area, silhouetted against the vast window as she spoke to her business partner.

Relief vied with irritation at the timing of the call. Relief that he had some time out—that kiss had felt like a reboot of a connection and he knew that the only way forward was to pull the plug. He wouldn't open up his heart to a woman who had already crushed it once. He didn't want to open up his heart to anyone, full stop. But he *had* wanted to continue the conversation because he'd seen doubt in her hazel eyes—doubt about his guilt—sensed he'd verged on a breakthrough.

He looked back at Isobel and saw by her frown and the way she was gesturing as she spoke that there was a problem.

'Clara, I'll figure something out and call you back. Just hold tight.'

'What's wrong?' he asked.

'One of my clients, Lucy—a bride-to-be—is having a bit of a meltdown. It's a tricky wedding to co-ordinate. There's a lot of family wrangling because they all have different opinions. They keep changing their minds about everything—venue, food, clothes, colours, flowers. Anyway, it's the wedding rehearsal the day after tomorrow; it's all falling apart a bit and they want me to go. But that's not the only problem.'

'Go ahead.'

'We've got a new client who wants to book us for a big event. She's been let down by someone else so wants to meet Clara ASAP. Preferably the day after tomorrow. It could be a really lucrative ongoing relationship.'

'Where's the rehearsal?'

'Cheltenham.'

'That's only a bit over an hour away.' Jake considered the problem; the solution seemed easy enough. 'Then you need to go.'

'I can't go. What about Emily? I can't take her with me. Not on my own.'

'I get that. I'll come as well. I'll look after Emily whilst you look after the client. You said you and Clara used to take Nat to things.'

'This is different. I promised Caro *I* would look after Emily—so that is what I need to do.'

'Caro asked both of us to look after Emily. I don't think Caro would object, especially when you're in the vicinity.'

'Nope. It wouldn't feel right. You're the security detail. I'm the hands-on one.'

'That's not set in stone. I'm sure you would do your best to protect Emily and I can be hands-on...' He broke off as he saw her small frown, sensing her hesitation. 'What?'

She shrugged and her forehead scrunched in question. 'Can you? I mean, you haven't shown any interest in Emily at all so far.'

That stung. 'That's not fair. Or true.'

She shook her head. 'Sorry. That came out wrong. I totally believe if anyone threatened her you would step in. I believe you care intensely about her safety. I meant you haven't shown any hands-on interest in her. As an individual. You haven't interacted with her. You haven't even held her.'

A quick search of his memory showed him that Isobel was right and a funny little knot of unease tugged inside him. 'Only because I have no experience with babies so it made more sense for you to look after her. It doesn't mean I can't look after her.'

'It's not that easy.'

'I get that and I'm not suggesting you simply hand her over. We have a whole day tomorrow where you can show me the ropes. Plus you'll be around on rehearsal day.'

Isobel chewed her bottom lip and he could sense her reluctance, guessing it went against the grain to accept a favour from him. But this wasn't only about her; this was about her business, about Clara, about Lucy, and he wasn't surprised when she gave a small nod.

'If you're sure, then let's give it a try. Starting tomorrow morning, you're in charge. But I'll be right next to you.'

'I'll look forward to it.' The words fell so easily from his lips, yet the after-effects rippled through the air, shimmered into the elephant in the room that had been banished by Clara's phone call. That kiss.

Isobel sighed. 'Look. About what happened earlier. The kiss—can we just forget it? It shouldn't have happened—it won't happen again. Let's delete it from our memory banks.'

'I'll try, but I don't think it's that easy. Think about what I said, Isobel. I don't think you could kiss me like that if you truly believe I cheated on you. I'm telling the truth about Anna.'

She said nothing, looking away from him out into the darkness of the night, illuminated by moonbeams. 'Let's just focus on Emily for now.'

* * *

The following morning Jake opened his eyes and identified a knot of anxiety in his stomach. He swung himself out of bed and frowned. He didn't do anxiety—not since he was a child, when he'd figured out the best way to control anxiety was to control his own destiny. Instead of living in his father's chaotic house, where he had no idea what was happening from one minute to the next, he'd asked to go to boarding school.

His father's relief had matched his own. 'Sure. Which one do you want?' had been Charles Cartwright's response.

From then on Jake hadn't looked back, and now he was on the cusp of control of Cartwright itself.

So there was no need for anxiety now. Looking after Emily wouldn't be a problem—it was simply a matter of learning how to do it. A quick shower, pulling on jeans and a top, and he emerged into the living area just as Isobel entered, Emily in her arms.

'You ready?' she asked.

'Um…' He could feel his already tenuous confidence desert him as he saw how Isobel held Emily—the baby looked so snug and cosy and safe and loved. How was he going to give Emily those same vibes? He was pretty sure he'd never received them—maybe he quite simply wasn't wired to do this. Maybe that was why he hadn't instinctively wanted to interact with Emily.

'Jake?' She moved towards him, clearly ready to hand Emily over.

'Yup.' Jeez. He could feel a bead of moisture on his temple. 'Though maybe you should feed her first—if she's hungry that may be best.'

'I think she'll be fine.' She met his gaze. 'Question is, are you?'

'Of course I am.'

'You look like you've seen a ghost or something. What's wrong?'

'Noth—' He broke off. 'I don't know.' He gave a half laugh. 'I didn't expect it to be so… scary. I mean, she's so tiny. What if I drop her?' After all, being in control of your own destiny was all very well—being responsible for someone else was different. Suddenly, all the things that could go wrong crowded into his mind. 'What if I hold her and she starts to cry?'

'Then it won't be personal.' Now he flinched as a locked-down memory suddenly shot free and impacted him so hard he nearly faltered.

Nothing personal. That was what his mother had said. She'd begun to cry, silent tears snaking down her cheeks.

'I'm sorry. So sorry. But I had to save my

brother. I swear to you, Jake, it was nothing personal.'

'Are you OK?' Isobel's hazel eyes glinted with concern now. 'You look like you've seen a ghost.'

'I'm fine.' He forced a smile. 'Maybe a little nervous.' But the words sounded stilted and as he looked at Emily something stirred in him, something he didn't understand. Emotions conflicted inside him—the desire to hold the baby and a sudden…sadness.

'Then let's take it slowly.' Isobel carefully held Emily towards him. 'You ready?' she asked.

'I'm ready.'

'Here.'

Heart pounding, Jake accepted Emily, careful to support her head.

Deep breaths.

He looked down at Emily, held her safe and close; he could smell the warm, milky baby smell, powder and baby shampoo. Emily flailed her hands, grabbed his finger and he would swear something shifted in his chest; a strange heat enveloped him, awe that this baby was so trusting, so dependent, so vulnerable. And it did twist his heart, made him wonder how his mother could have walked away from him, then stayed away.

'I signed an agreement saying I'd give you up. How could I have fought the Cartwright family against that? I told myself that you would have your own life, a happy life. And—' She'd made a helpless gesture around the room. *'Then I met my husband.'*

He'd got it—she'd made herself a new life—one she wanted to protect, he'd realised as he saw her furtive glance at her watch, then at the door. So he'd left.

The memories stabbed into him one by one and he forced himself to remain still, feeling Isobel's gaze on him. He had to lock this down; he despised the feeling that somehow, without his permission, emotions had crept up on him, caught him unaware. Emotions did not control him, he controlled them.

This must stop now.

'Jake?'

He looked up at Isobel. 'She's lovely,' he said. 'And I would have happily looked after her.' The words rang hollow in his ears. 'But I've had a better idea, better for Emily and easier for you. I'll ask Maria to come down for the day and come with us. It makes more sense. You will be more relaxed because you'll be more confident that Emily is being properly looked after.' He forced himself to smile, an easy practised smile. 'So you're off the hook—

having to show me how to look after Emily. You may as well feed her whilst I call Maria.'

He stood up carefully, took one last look at Emily. *Sorry, little one*, he thought. *It's not your fault you simply trigger too much emotion inside me*. She made him feel weak and vulnerable, as he must have been nigh on thirty years ago.

'Here you go,' he said and looked at Isobel expectantly.

There was a pause and then she shook her head. 'Actually, would you hold onto her whilst I go and get her milk?'

And with that she headed to the kitchenette, quite literally leaving him holding the baby.

As Isobel took the milk out of the fridge and warmed it up, her mind raced. The rational, logical part of her brain told her to leave it—if Jake didn't want to look after Emily that was none of her business. The idea of asking Maria was a good one and did solve the problem—provided Lucy didn't mind Isobel arriving accompanied by two companions and a baby. Which she wouldn't.

So it was all good, right? But it wasn't—Isobel had enough demons on her own back and she could recognise the symptoms. Whatever had happened to Jake just then, as he'd held Emily, had been important—his grey eyes had held the darkest of shadows, his expression haunted. He had been a man in pain.

Picking up the milk, she made her decision and headed back to Jake, who was standing exactly where she'd left him, Emily still safely enclosed in his arms, and for a moment she stilled, watched him. She saw how carefully he held the baby, and warmth touched her chest. Then Emily whimpered, a precursor to a full cry as she waited for her milk.

Jake's lips tightened and she sensed his tension, recognised it as panic. Wordlessly, she held the bottle out. 'She's just hungry. Why don't you feed her?'

Now he frowned. 'I thought I explained—I am going to call Maria.'

'I get that. But that doesn't mean you can't feed Emily.'

'I know that.'

His gaze met hers and she held it steadily. 'I think you're scared. Are you?'

He hesitated and she felt her heart twist at the expression in his eyes—a look of almost bemusement as he looked down at Emily. 'I'll take her,' she offered. 'But I'd like to know what's going on.' As she took Emily from him she sensed his relief and his withdrawal. 'I'd like to help.'

'I don't need help.'

'OK then. But I'd still like to know. We agreed that this time together would be used for closure, for talking through what went wrong with us.'

'This has nothing to do with what went wrong with us.'

'Maybe, maybe not. But I think it's something important to you, something important in your life.'

He shook his head. 'I've dealt with it and moved on.'

'You admit there is an "it". If you've dealt with it, then prove it. Feed Emily. If you've moved on from it you may as well tell me what it is.'

To her surprise, and perhaps to his, a small smile quirked his lips and for a second amusement glinted through the clouds in his grey eyes. 'What?' she asked.

'It's you. I'd forgotten how tenacious you are and how earnest.'

Tenacious and earnest—the two words pricked her feminine pride even as she nodded acknowledgement. 'I'll take that as a compliment and an admission I'm right.'

Jake's shoulders lifted in a shrug. 'Fine. I had a reaction to Emily.' Again the smile, but this time there was no amusement. 'I made it sound like an allergy. Maybe it is like that— she triggered something inside me.' He shifted from foot to foot, his discomfort at this conversation more than evident.

'I don't understand.'

'I'm not sure I do either. I think Emily reminded me of my own past. My mother left me when I was a baby. Not like Caro left Emily. I mean she packed her bags and left me in the hospital. I was only a couple of days old.'

Isobel could feel her skin go cold as her brain struggled to understand the words.

'I didn't see her again until I was eighteen. Someone presumably took me home from the hospital, but I don't know who it was.'

'Your father?'

'No. It couldn't have been him because he took off on a nine-month cruise.'

'But who looked after you?' Unconsciously, she realised her hold on Emily had tightened and she relaxed, saw that Emily had finished her bottle.

'I don't know. I do know that my grandfather stepped in when I was nine months old. I lived with him after that.'

Isobel burped Emily, dropped a kiss on her head and then carefully placed her down on her play mat, making sure she was happy and seemingly intent on whacking the cloth animals that dangled from the bar. Then she turned her full attention to Jake. 'But those first nine months?'

'Well, obviously, someone looked after me, maybe a nanny, maybe some well-wishing friend. Who knows?' Jake frowned. 'In the end, who cares?'

'I do.' Isobel's voice was low and without thinking she reached out and took his hand, interlaced her fingers with his, her whole being heated with sheer outrage on Jake's behalf. Because she did care—of course she did—she would care about any baby abandoned by the person who was meant to nurture them. Even her own mother had kept her, done her best. Imperceptibly, she shifted closer to Jake and in that moment she knew that whilst all abandoned babies mattered, this was personal. It was Jake she was thinking of, imagining him as a small defenceless baby, handed over to an anonymous carer.

'It doesn't really matter. It happened. I survived. I moved on.'

'It does matter.' Her hand gripped his so hard he glanced down involuntarily and she relaxed. 'Sorry. I am just so livid on your behalf. How could they?'

He shrugged, but he kept his hand in hers and she hoped the connection gave him the comfort that she sensed he would take as unwanted pity if she put it in words. 'They did what they did, but in the end I had food, clothes, a roof over my head, an expensive education and plenty of money in the bank. It all worked out. No big deal.'

'It is a huge deal and you know it. Or at least your body does. Isn't that what you said to me yesterday—you told me to listen to my body. Maybe right now your body is telling you that it does matter and maybe you haven't dealt with it.'

'I have dealt with it.'

'Then why won't you feed Emily? Or interact with her?'

'Maybe I'm not a baby person.'

'Maybe you aren't. But perhaps you should give yourself a chance to find out. What your parents did to you sucks and it is holding you back from bonding with this gorgeous small, innocent being. You can change that. If you want to. Yes, it means you may have to face some emotions but surely it's worth it.'

There was a long silence. 'I'm not really an emotional kind of guy,' he said eventually.

And she couldn't blame him—no wonder he didn't want to think about what his parents had done. She truly couldn't comprehend how his mother could have walked away and how rejected that must make him feel. But for his father to have acted in the same way was a double whammy that must have put salt in the wound.

'There is nothing wrong with emotion.' Jake raised an eyebrow and she knew that he thought there was everything wrong with emotion. 'Not when you get the chance to bond with Emily.'

Another silence as he looked down at Emily. 'I guess I can try,' he said finally.

'Then let's take her out for the morning,' Isobel suggested. 'Just to the park to feed the ducks. She seemed to like the ducks yesterday. I'll get her stuff together and you keep an eye on her. All you have to do is watch her and if she cries pick her up. Or sing to her. Or wave one of her toys—she likes that.'

'OK. Got it.'

Isobel turned round before she left the room, saw how intently he was looking at Emily, saw him tentatively reach out and stroke the baby's downy head and something melted inside her, made her feel gooey and warm.

Whoa. Careful here, Iz.

Gooey warmth was great when it came to chocolate brownies—not when it came to feelings, especially for Jake. She'd got her life on track, made a niche for herself where she fitted in, where she was happy. Most important of all, she was heading towards security and independence and safety. No way would she forget that.

CHAPTER SEVEN

JAKE WAVED A brightly coloured, crinkly-sounding toy that he thought might be an elephant at Emily and she kicked her legs and smiled as if he had performed the most amazing feat in the universe. And in truth he felt as if he'd done just that. The door opened and he looked up as Isobel re-entered briskly, holding up the sling.

'Let's get you buckled up,' she said cheerfully.

He rose, oh, so careful not to let his feet anywhere near Emily, and Isobel moved towards him until she was so close he could smell the tantalising apple scent of her shampoo and he had to resist the urge to lean in and inhale her, to run his hand through the silken tresses. Quickly, he took the sling from her, unsure whether the fleeting brush of their hands was deliberate or accidental. All he did know was that the touch impacted him out of all proportion. That her closeness dizzied him.

Enough.

He seemed to be losing his grip on *all* his emotions at an alarming rate—and it would stop now. Stepping back, he studied the sling.

'You need to slip your arms in and then adjust the straps. You can carry Emily forward-facing—that way she can see what's going on, but she's close to you so she feels reassured and cared for.'

'How's this?'

Now she did step forward, stood on tiptoe and tugged on the straps, quickly ran her hands round his waist to check the sling was correctly secured. Her hair tickled his chin and he bit back a small moan, knew he must not unravel now.

'Looking good,' she said and he noted her quickened breathing.

'I aim to please.' For Pete's sake. What had that been? Banter? Had he been flirting? Teasing? Panicking? That was it. Nerves over Emily had somehow affected his sanity.

Isobel picked Emily up and carefully placed her in the sling as he stood stock still. He felt his lips curve into a smile as Emily kicked her chubby legs as if inciting him to get a move on.

The walk to the park had a surreal feel, the birdsong louder, the flowers brighter, the clouds whiter. 'It's almost as if I'm seeing the world through Emily's eyes,' he realised.

Isobel nodded. 'That's exactly it.'

They continued in comfortable silence until they got to the park and approached the lake. A few more steps and she looked up at him. 'How are you feeling?'

He considered the question. 'Part of me is terrified that I'll mess it up but most of me is feeling great.' It was true; this moment was a happy one and the realisation gave him a momentary qualm. He, Jake Cartwright, on the cusp of pulling off the coup he'd worked towards for all his adult life, was walking through a park to feed the ducks with a baby and a woman he'd believed he'd exorcised from his life and he was...happy.

Some of that happiness was brought about by the closeness of the baby—her utterly new and innocent perceptions of the world, her trust and belief that that world held safety and love and—milk and ducks and hugs and wellbeing. The knowledge that right now she trusted him to provide that was huge.

'I'm glad because you're doing great,' Isobel said with the sweetest of smiles that encompassed both Jake *and* Emily.

'It's made me think as well that the nanny, or whoever it was who looked after me, maybe she was OK. I mean, Emily only just met us and she seems happy, right?'

Isobel nodded. 'Definitely,' she said as Emily gave a little gurgle that truly did seem to indicate joy with the world.

They whiled away an hour throwing bread to the ducks and walking, letting the sun warm their faces, watching children playing on the swings, building sandcastles in the sandpits.

'I brought a picnic,' she said after a while. 'You can feed Emily and then she can have her nap on a blanket in the shade whilst we eat.'

'Good thinking.' So that was what he did. He settled himself against the trunk of a shady willow tree and under Isobel's instruction put the bottle to Emily's lips. Emotion rocked him again. This act of providing sustenance brought home the fact that Emily could not do this for herself, was dependent on them.

The baby guzzled happily, so trusting and peaceful, her tiny hands reaching up to touch the bottle, her eyes already closing, her satisfaction so evident it touched his heart with warmth.

'What now?' he whispered.

'You have to burp her. Just hold her up and pat her back gently.'

It should have been simple but it flummoxed him and Isobel moved next to him, her warmth giving him confidence as she showed him, his feeling of achievement as Emily emitted a belch ridiculously strong. 'You're a natural,' Isobel said and the words gave him a buzz, a glow. 'I think she'll sleep now. Pop her down on the blanket.' He lowered Emily gently and watched as the baby gave a small murmur and then closed her eyes.

Isobel unpacked her rucksack. 'I've got cheese sandwiches.'

'Sounds great. I'm ravenous.'

As they ate he watched her for a moment, looked at Emily and hauled in a breath. 'Do you think I could look after her tomorrow? At the rehearsal?'

'Absolutely I do.' Her smile was wide and contagious and he returned it as his gaze absorbed her beauty.

'Thank you for persuading me to take a chance with Emily.'

'I'm so glad you did. You have truly been brilliant with her. Calm and nurturing and gentle and—safe.' Her emphasis on the word told him that there were different ways of keeping a baby safe and that he'd fulfilled them all. 'And thank you for telling me about your parents. I know that must have been hard and, for the record, they missed out. Big time.' Then she leaned forward and kissed his cheek; for a second his body froze, the scent of jasmine, the nearness of her jolted him and he revelled in the tickle of her silky hair against his skin.

Then he moved, shifted so that his gaze met hers and he saw a spark ignite as her hazel eyes darkened. And then she tumbled into his arms, and oh, so slowly, so very tantalisingly slowly, he cupped her face in his hands, his palms against her cheeks feeling so sensuous, and his eyes met hers directly, wanting to make sure this was what she wanted too, that this was their choice, their decision.

And she didn't hesitate—she leaned towards him and brushed her lips against his, the touch ephemeral, and yet the sensation that rushed inside him was exquisite in its intensity. Now he couldn't stop the momentum of this instant of time and he didn't even want to try.

Then he kissed her, plundered her lips, unleashing a riot of sensation. He tasted the traces of chocolate, as desire rocketed and surged through his veins.

The moment felt timeless and it was only the sudden disappearance of the sun behind the clouds that pulled them from the fugue of desire. The sudden morph from hot to cold shadowed his skin as she pulled away from him, her hazel eyes wide, still fogged with desire.

He leant back against the solid reality of the

tree trunk as she rocked back on her haunches, their breathing ragged, and he stared at her, knew he was in trouble. That had been too intense, too overwhelming; it had left his body tied in knots of desire, aching with frustration.

'We shouldn't have done that, should we?' she asked.

'Probably not. But I don't care.' Because, despite the knowledge that it had been both reckless and foolhardy, right now he couldn't bring himself to regret it. And that was more troublesome than anything else. It was time to get a grip.

'Well, I do.' She closed her eyes. 'I don't know what's going on here but we have to stop it. It's not…what I want. It's all confusing enough as it is. I don't know what to think any more—about Anna and you, about the truth, about what's going on here. And kissing you—I'm scared it's messing with my head, my judgement.'

Hope spiked inside him that maybe she was beginning to believe she'd got it wrong all those years ago. 'I'm sorry,' he said. 'I didn't mean to muddy the water or blur the lines. You're right. We're looking for closure—reigniting our physical connection isn't going to achieve that.' He managed a smile. 'However tempting it may be.'

'No, it isn't.' Her hazel eyes were troubled now. 'No more kisses.'

'No more kisses,' he agreed.

The next morning Isobel watched as Jake strapped Emily into her car seat, saw the deft movements and felt a glow of satisfaction, of happiness at his confidence and the way he had bonded with Emily. However confused she was right now, and inner turmoil had kept her awake most of the night, she was glad that Jake had shared some of his past with her, thrilled he'd connected with Emily.

But now she had to think of herself—events were swerving out of her control. The idea had been to gain an insight into why he had betrayed her and get closure. Instead of insight, all she had were doubts—the more she heard, the more she saw, the more she believed he had told her the truth all those years ago. That Anna had lied. As for closure, she was pretty damned sure kissing was not on the closure agenda. Let alone kissing him twice.

But now she needed to focus on work, on the rehearsal. Not Jake.

So, once they were on the way, she was relieved when he said, 'Tell me about the wedding rehearsal.'

'We're heading to Lucy's mum's house. It

will be a bit chaotic. Lucy will be there, so will her mum, her two sisters and the chief bridesmaid. I'm going to have a catch-up, make sure she's happy with everything, and then we'll head to the church for the rehearsal.'

'Right, so what do I do?'

'I've explained you're coming with Emily and they are fine with that. So just hover in the background and try to radiate calm and goodwill and hopefully that will rub off on everyone else.'

'Got it.'

An hour later he pulled into a driveway that fronted a large Georgian house. 'Right. Let's do this.'

They reached the front door, where Isobel took a deep breath, focused and then knocked. Seconds later the door was pulled open.

'Isobel.'

'Hello, Natasha.' Isobel smiled at the mother of the bride, a woman in her early sixties, made-up to perfection, her hair a perfect honey-ash bob, pale pink lipstick on a thin-lipped smile and blue eyes that were harder than ice.

'Thank heavens you're here. Clara has been acceptable but we need you. You can manage Lucy.'

Isobel smiled. 'It's always hard to come into

a wedding plan halfway through but I know Clara has enjoyed working with you and we really appreciate that you've accommodated us.' It was diplomatic and made it very clear that she and Clara were a team. 'But I'm also really pleased to be here for the rehearsal and thank you so much for saying Jake and Emily can come too.' She turned to Jake. 'Jake, this is Natasha Redwood, mother of the bride.'

Natasha looked at Emily. 'So sweet,' she said in a tone of voice that didn't indicate any such thing. 'Please come through.'

They stepped onto a polished wooden floor and Isobel grinned as Lucy hurtled down the stairs. 'Isobel!' the redhead shrieked. 'I am *so* glad to see you. Everything is a mess, my hair looks like straw and I've eaten my own weight in chocolate—and I don't know if the dress is right, and—'

'Lucy, it's all going to be fine, I promise. You look fantastic and anyway, Jim would love you even if you were quadruple your weight with no hair.' She hugged the other woman. 'And today will be fun and our opportunity to make sure you're all happy with everything. And if you aren't happy I'll fix it.'

'Well, actually, I do have some things to talk to you about—' The words were synchronised as both mother and daughter said the same thing, and then both launched into a litany of problems and counter problems.

'OK. It sounds like we need a good catch-up. Would it be possible for Jake to perhaps take Emily into the garden or—?'

Now Lucy turned to Jake. 'I am so sorry. You must think I'm rude or mad or both! I'm not, honestly—I'm just afflicted by wedding fever and Isobel here is the only person who can bring my temperature down. In real life, I am completely normal—I work in an art gallery, I'm good with people and I have an eye for colour which has completely deserted me. And I'm talking too much.'

'Yes, you are,' her mum intervened. 'Honestly, Lucy, sometimes you're no different from when you were six. No matter how hard I've tried. Anyway—' Natasha sighed '—Jake, if you would like to take the baby into the conservatory, that would be fine.'

'I'm happy to look after him,' purred a voice suddenly and a tall, svelte blonde entered the room and glided towards him. 'I'm Julia; I'm a bridesmaid. Here to be helpful.' She smiled at Jake. 'I love being helpful.'

Isobel froze in mid-sentence and turned, watching as Julia sashayed over to Jake. How had she not noticed before how stunning the blonde woman was? Her hair fell down her back, she was tall, slim, elegant, with endless legs and a plummy voice redolent of a private education.

Not that it mattered, yet a stab of sheer envy knifed Isobel.

Envy? Of what, for Pete's sake? The other woman's gorgeousness? The fact that she had headed straight for Jake? The fact that Julia was in the Anna mould? So bloody what? Just hours ago, she'd questioned whether Jake had even slept with Anna. But that wasn't the point—the point was that Anna had been Jake's type.

'That would be wonderful, Julia,' Natasha said. 'You show Jake the conservatory and we'll all head to the church after our pow-wow.'

For a treacherous second Isobel was tempted to request that Julia join the 'pow-wow' and pressed her lips together to stop the suggestion from emerging. That way lay madness—she must not, should not, would not walk that road. She had no stake in Jake's love life—perhaps Julia would be perfect for one of his short and sweet relationships. The thought caused another tinge of green and she knew this had to stop.

'Great,' she said. 'Shall we convene in the dining room?'

Out of the corner of her eye she saw Julia usher Jake out of the room. 'What an adorable baby.'

Again negativity twisted her tummy and she forced a smile to her lips. 'OK, let's get started.'

Jake watched as Isobel left the room, with only the most fleeting of backward glances. There was a smile on her lips but he would swear something flashed across her hazel eyes—an expression that he'd seen before, though he couldn't quite place it.

He turned his attention to Julia, who had moved forward in a gust of perfume to tickle Emily's cheek. 'Such a sweet little baby,' she gushed at Emily, who stared wide-eyed at her for a few seconds and then emitted a wail that propelled the blonde woman backwards. 'Babies usually love me,' she said.

'She's probably hungry, or not used to a new person,' Jake said diplomatically, aware of Isobel's instruction to radiate goodwill.

'I'll show you to the conservatory. Would you like tea or coffee? Anything at all.'

'I'm fine, thank you.'

Jake was aware of a wish that Julia would go and join the others—give him time to focus on Emily, make sure he was doing everything right, but instead she seemed far more interested in making conversation and he duly complied until Natasha appeared in the doorway.

'Julia, we need you—come and try to talk some sense into Lucy about her hair.'

'Hope to see you later.' Julia blew a kiss and sashayed from the room.

'Peace at last,' Jake said to Emily, who was lying on the floor studying her toes as if they held the answer to the universe. 'In here, anyway. Goodness knows what is happening with Isobel.'

He took the baby's gurgle to be a sympathetic response and sat down next to her until she started to grizzle. Quickly, he picked her up and started to feed her.

Isobel entered as Emily emitted an enormous burp.

'You wouldn't think someone so tiny could make such a loud noise,' he commented.

'No.' The syllable was clipped and he couldn't see so much as a hint of a smile on her face.

'Tough pow-wow?' he asked sympathetically.

'It was fine. Is Emily OK?' Now she did smile as she headed to the baby and stroked her cheek. 'Hello, poppet,' she cooed.

'Everything is fine. What's happening now?'

'We're headed to the church. Natasha says you can stay here if you like.' Her hazel eyes studied him, almost as if this were some sort of test.

'I'm happy to take you.'

Her eyes narrowed and he sensed that had been the wrong answer though, for the life of him, he couldn't figure out why. 'Why?'

'I thought you may want a bit of a break in the car. And I assumed you'd want to be near Emily.'

That wrong-footed her, though again he was at sea. 'Oh. OK. Then that would be great. Thank you.'

In the car he tried again to instigate a conversation, but gave up when she answered in monosyllables. Perhaps Isobel needed quiet to regroup, yet the silence was edged with discomfort.

Once they arrived at the church Isobel turned and gave him a quick perfunctory smile. 'Thank you. Feel free to come inside and watch…proceedings.' An emphasis on the last word. With that she slipped from the car and headed towards the pretty stone church, where it looked as though an argument had broken out, both Lucy and Natasha gesticulating, the sound of raised voices carried on the still spring air.

Jake decided to wait before exiting the car. He watched as Isobel approached the mother and daughter, spoke to them both, clearly restoring calm before they entered the picturesque church.

He frowned, trying to work out what on earth was going on, aware of a sense of both bewilderment and hurt and a nagging sense that he should be able to figure this out. They'd been getting on—getting on too well if anything—so it didn't make sense for Isobel to suddenly turn a cold shoulder. Unless it was her way of trying to reverse the damage done, offset the heat and smoulder and warmth. Perhaps it was a good strategy. Yet instinct told him it was something else.

A noise from Emily jolted him from his thoughts and he turned to soothe her before climbing out of the car. A few minutes later, Emily in his arms, Jake slipped in the back of the church and stood in one of the pews.

He watched as Lucy walked down the aisle, saw Jim waiting for her, saw the goofy smile on the soon-to-be groom's face and realised that perhaps he wasn't to be pitied that much. In truth, there was something beautiful about the rehearsal.

He stepped further in the shadows as Lucy and Jim walked back down the aisle hand in hand, the bride-to-be smiling up at her chosen partner in life with a smile so full of happiness that for an instant he nearly bought into the whole wedding malarkey.

Then he shook his head at his own idiocy—marriage wasn't about the walk up and down an aisle—it was about being able to pull together as a partnership for years and years.

Before he could exit the church Julia headed towards him. 'Hello, Tiger.'

For a moment he wondered if she was speaking to Emily then realised this was directed at him.

'Hey,' he said warily.

'Did you enjoy it?'

Before he could answer, Emily began to grizzle. Jake decided that it could be Julia's perfume the baby disliked, the musky scent a little too heavy and cloying.

'It was sweet enough, I suppose.' She answered her own question. 'But I won't be lining up to catch the bouquet.'

There was a pause that Jake realised he was supposed to fill.

'Why's that?' he asked.

'I'm fresh out of a relationship and I'm looking for some fun. And you look like a fun guy. I'm not usually so forward but what the heck. Here's my number.' She pushed a piece of paper into his hand and then turned and walked away before he could say anything at all.

Jake contemplated the paper and then he slipped it into his back pocket; in truth, he wasn't sure what to do next. He could hardly follow her out and explain he wasn't interested. And he definitely wasn't. Julia may be up for short and sweet but he felt nothing for her; there hadn't been even a glimmer of—anything. How could there be when Isobel was in the picture?

A warning bell began to clang at the back of his mind; he and Isobel were pursuing closure. In a few days she would no longer be in the picture and he would be preparing to walk into the most important meeting of his life—the board meeting that would bring him what he had striven for over the past four years. Control of the Cartwright business.

A quick scan showed no bin in the vicinity so he shrugged, shoved the note in his pocket, exited the church and headed towards Isobel.

'I need to chat to the photographer, then we're good to go.'

'We're ready when you are.'

There was now a definite coolness to her voice as, she took Emily from him. 'Hello, sweetheart. I missed you.' Now her gaze softened as she held the tiny baby to her.

But when she turned her eyes back to him he could see glaciers in her eyes. Jake frowned slightly as his mind raced, running over the day's events, trying to see them through Isobel's eyes, and suddenly the penny dropped. But now wasn't the time to discuss it, not whilst Emily was awake.

Isobel stared at the pasta dish Jake had made, telling herself it would be childish to refuse to eat it. She had to get a grip. So what if Julia liked Jake? Come to that, so what if Jake liked Julia? Isobel certainly had no hold on Jake at all—a couple of kisses, a couple of *mistakes* didn't mean anything. Yet…it rankled, goddamn it, it *hurt* that those kisses clearly hadn't rocked his world the way they had hers. Otherwise how could he be interested in Julia? And he must be interested—they'd spent long enough together in the church. Plus, the woman was gorgeous, smart, fun, wealthy… On and on rolled the list.

'That looks delicious,' she managed, even as her appetite left the table. 'Thank you.'

Jake raised an eyebrow as she served herself a fraction of her usual portion.

'Is it OK?' he asked.

'It looks delicious.' And it did. The sauce was simple yet aromatic, the ingredients all favourites of hers—tomatoes, basil, olives and capers.

'I thought you'd like it. And you definitely deserve it. You did an amazing job today. From Chaos to Calm—that could be your slogan.'

'Thank you.' This was better. Normal conversation. 'You did brilliantly with Emily. Was it all right?'

'It was fine. Great. I enjoyed it; she's a very edifying conversationalist.'

'She liked Julia.'

Really, Isobel? Really?

Aware of his grey eyes studying her expression, she forced herself to relax.

He shook his head. 'Not really. I don't think she liked her perfume. Bit too cloying.'

'Julia's nice, though, Lots of fun, according to Lucy.'

Stop it, Isobel.

But she couldn't. 'What did you think of her?' The attempt at casual fell flatter than flatbread.

'Why do you ask?'

'No reason. Just curious. Making conversation. She seemed interested in you.'

'Is that a problem?'

'Of course not.' Once the lie escaped her

lips she knew she had to back it up; somehow she had to make it into the truth. She loathed the fact that she did mind, that she detested the idea of Jake and Julia together. 'I—' she jutted her chin '—I just thought…if you were interested in her maybe I could…tell you more about her.' This was getting worse and worse; the idea of helping Jake get together with Julia was excruciating. That realisation itself made her want to kick herself round the cottage.

'Isobel—' he raised a hand '—you don't have to do that. I am not interested in Julia. At all.'

'You aren't?' Her voice came out ridiculously small and she shook her head in annoyance.

'Nope.' His frown deepened as he studied her face and she dropped her gaze to her plate, forked up a mouthful of pasta. 'Iz? Look at me. Why is that so hard to believe?'

There was a question she could answer. 'Oh, come on! The woman is beautiful. Blonde hair, legs to her armpits; she could be a model. In case you hadn't noticed, she is also super intelligent, with an excellent background. I think she even has a first-class degree from Oxford.' A replica of Anna, though she didn't say it. 'Julia is the sort of woman you could easily take to yacht parties or jet off to the Bahamas with.'

'That's all great. Problem is, I don't want to take her. I'm not interested. If I were I'd tell you.'

Isobel closed her eyes, trying hard to separate irrational feelings from genuine ones. Trying to figure out the best thing to say or do. She opened her eyes and studied his face, the fine mix of strength and masculine beauty of his features—the squareness of his jaw, the jut of his nose, even the strong curve of his brows. It occurred to her that this was a man you could trust, he had no reason to lie to her and he wouldn't even if he did.

Looking at him, she gave a small nod. 'OK. I believe you.'

'Good.' Now he smiled at her and she smiled back. The moment seemed to stretch into a timeless chasm, and then her phone rang.

It was an unfamiliar number and she grabbed it, heard the caller's voice. 'Isobel?'

'Caro? It's me.'

CHAPTER EIGHT

JAKE STILLED, INSTANTLY clearing his mind of their conversation, and watched Isobel's expression.

'Caro, are you OK…? Yes, Emily is fine. Super-fine and absolutely adorable… What's happening…? Jake's here. I'm going to put you on loudspeaker.'

She suited action to word, placing the phone on the table, and they both leaned forward slightly.

'I'm going to meet with Martin tomorrow.'

He and Isobel exchanged glances. 'Is that a good plan?' he asked.

'I have to meet him. I can't run and hide for ever. I'm going to get him to agree to leave us alone.'

'How?' Isobel asked as her face creased with worry.

'I'll explain I'll get a legal injunction, that if

he comes anywhere near me he'll end up back in jail. I've got a lawyer.'

'Then maybe the lawyer should handle this,' Jake suggested.

'Where are you meeting him?' Isobel asked.

There was a hesitation. 'At his house.'

'Why not at the lawyer's office?' Jake asked.

'Because Martin refused to do that.'

'Caro—' Isobel's voice held a plea now '—it's not safe to go and meet Martin alone.'

'I haven't got a choice.'

'Yes, you do. Meet somewhere else. In a public space.'

'He won't do that. And I have to see him. I have to get him to promise to leave us alone. Otherwise—'

'I know, Caro. I know. But you have to take someone with you.'

'It will be OK. I have to do this my way. I'll let you know how it goes and then I'll come for Emily. Please give her a huge hug from me and tell her I will see her soon. And thank you, both of you, for looking after her.'

With that she was gone.

Isobel's face had paled to chalk; she placed her hand in a protective curve over her tummy and stared at him wide-eyed. 'I can't let her go in there alone. It's not safe...'

'I don't get it.' Jake started to pace. 'Why is

she seeing him at his house? Why won't she take the lawyer with her? Why doesn't she insist he—?'

'Because it doesn't work like that!' Isobel's voice was taut; her words whipped through the air and halted him in his tracks. 'She can't.'

'Why not?' Frustration laced his tone— he knew Caro, she was smart, funny, a bit quiet but definitely not stupid. And this was stupid—to go and meet a violent man in his house, alone. Isobel must see that.

'You don't understand what it's like, Jake.' Now she was pacing too, each step nervy and terrified and scared.

'Then tell me. Tell me why she is walking into danger.' Frustration fuelled his anger. 'It's a stupid thing to do.'

'Don't be so judgemental. It's not that easy for Caro.'

He studied the fear in her hazel eyes and saw its depth, but also saw an understanding that he knew was born of experience.

Now he ceased his strides, stood and leant back on the kitchen counter and instinct made his voice gentle. 'OK. Explain.' He sensed Isobel's fear for Caro had sent her to the edge of a personal hell.

She halted in front of him. 'Caro is scared of him and she is trying to confront that fear. But she is also trying to please him, to set a scene where he won't hurt her. It's what abusers do—they induce this strange double-stranded reaction of fear and hope. Caro knows what it's like to be hurt and she knows what Martin is capable of, but she also hopes that this time he'll be nice, that he'll give her what she wants. But he won't. We have to stop her.'

Reaching out, he took her hands in his. 'You've experienced this, haven't you?' The thought imploded in his brain and he hoped that he was wrong, knew that he wasn't.

Isobel hesitated and then she nodded. 'My dad died when I was a baby. A year later my mum met Simon and he charmed her, made her believe he'd look after her and me. Turned out his methods of looking after people left a lot to be desired. I grew up in fear. That's what he thrived on, because fear gave him power. We never knew when he would flip, and all I cared about was not triggering his rage because he would take it out on Mum. Every time he hit her, my heart would break a little more and my fear would notch a little higher.' Jake could see that remembered pain and fear etched on her face and anger and sadness tightened his chest. 'My mother tried so hard to please him, lived in hope that somehow he would change. And that's how he messed with her head—because there were times when he would be loving and kind and then suddenly, wham, out of the blue he'd lose his rag.'

Each and every word, the vivid picture she painted, chilled his blood, hurt his very soul and he wished he knew what to say, wished he could go back in time and protect Isobel. 'What about you? Did he hurt you?'

'Yes, but mostly just bruises, not like he hurt Mum.' Her matter-of-fact tone was even worse than if she'd bemoaned her fate. 'But he would shout in my face, insult me... Worst of all, he would tell me it was my fault he had to hurt Mum. If I ever tried to protect her or stand up to him, he'd take it out on her and make me watch. He told me that if I went to the police he'd kill her. And I believed him.'

'Why didn't she leave?' He heard the anger in his own words and shook his head. 'Sorry.' Anger was the last thing she needed to hear right now, even if it wasn't directed at her. Yet the idea of Isobel, small and vulnerable and scared and hurt, rocked him with rage, twisted his chest with an ache of sadness.

'I'd beg her to leave. When I was older I found details of refuges and gave them to her—there were so many times when I told her we should just run and hide. But she couldn't. It's difficult to explain the hold he had over her; she was in thrall to him because he had her life in his hand. And somehow he made her believe that he loved her.' She spat out the last words with contempt.

His chest constricted as he imagined how appalling her childhood must have been. 'I know that nothing I say can change what happened to you, but I am so truly sorry that it did.'

She inhaled a deep breath. 'It's OK. I didn't tell you because I want pity.'

'That's good because I'm not offering pity. I'm offering admiration for the person you've become, for the bravery you must have shown to survive, and I'm offering compassion because no child should have to go through that.'

'Thank you.' But he could see she didn't believe his words, that her childhood had caused wounds that it would take way more than a few words to heal. He wondered if a part of her did believe Simon's words, that she blamed herself. So, because he didn't know what else to do or say, he moved forward and, hesitantly at first, wanting to give her the chance to move away, he put his arms around her.

For a moment she stiffened but then she relaxed into his hold and leant her cheek against his chest. So they stood for a few minutes whilst he tried to somehow convey sympathy and support and regret.

After a while she gently disengaged and looked up at him with a mixture of shyness and defensiveness on her face. 'Truly I didn't tell you that for sympathy. I told you because I wanted to explain why Caro is behaving how she is and how important it is that she doesn't go back to Martin. That she doesn't talk to him on her own.'

Compassion deepened as he realised how terrified Isobel must be for Caro, because she knew first-hand exactly how much damage Martin could do, both physically and mentally, to Caro. She knew too how Caro's actions could impact on Emily; Isobel must see herself in Emily, must want to protect the baby from growing up in fear as she had. He could only imagine the anguished tangle of her feelings and Jake couldn't help himself. Gently he cupped her face in his hands, felt the smooth silk of her skin, saw the tiny birthmark that dotted the top of one angular cheekbone, the length of her lashes.

'Whatever your reasons, I'm glad you told me. Now we need to figure out how to protect Caro.' For Caro's sake, but also for Isobel. He wanted—*needed*—to alleviate the fear in her hazel eyes. 'I'll go with her to Martin's, with

Stefan and three other security guards. And a lawyer.'

'Caro won't let you.'

'Yes, she will. Because if she doesn't I will take Emily to social services. Full stop.'

'But—'

There aren't any buts. I'm not bluffing—I will not risk Caro going back to Martin and trying to take Emily back. But I don't think it will come to that. I'm pretty sure Caro will agree. Hopefully, Martin will be intimidated, see that Caro has real protection now. Perhaps if she sees him back down it will help break his hold over her.'

Now Isobel smiled and he saw the relief in her stance. 'Thank you. And I agree—Caro won't risk Emily going into care. But it doesn't solve the problem long-term. You can't keep a security detail with her for ever.' Isobel frowned. 'We need somewhere safe for her to stay. Like a refuge. I couldn't persuade my mum but I will do my best to persuade Caro. I'll start researching now. Then I'll call Caro.' She moved closer to him. 'Thank you for doing this.'

'There is no need to thank me. I want to do this. For Emily. For Caro.' But also for Isobel; now he knew about her childhood he understood how deeply this must be affecting her.

How desperate she must be to prevent a repeat, how badly she must want to save both Emily and her best friend.

The following morning Isobel threw the duvet off, pulled it back on again, tried to snatch a few more minutes of elusive sleep. Uneasy dreams had agitated her night—fear for Caro and for Emily.

Enough. Far better to muster positive thoughts. Caro had agreed that Jake could come with her, had promised to bring her own lawyer. Jake would keep Caro safe. As long as Caro didn't go back to Martin. Because then she would lose Emily and that would send her friend spiralling downward, extinguish all hope and light. Without Emily, Caro would fall, give up, like Isobel's mum had when Isobel was taken into care. Guilt seeped through her being—she should have done *something* to stay with her mother, hidden the abuse better, not slipped up...

Pushing the dark thoughts away, she got up and fifteen minutes later she emerged into the living area where Jake sat and an additional fear twisted within her. 'You will take care?'

'Of course. I don't think Martin will try anything. He's just out of prison. There will be a lawyer present. And plenty of witnesses. All we need to do is deliver Caro's message—that he needs to stay away from Emily.'

Isobel nodded. 'And I have details of the refuge—Caro has agreed to talk about it. It was set up specifically to help mothers like Caro; it's a residential clinic for mothers and babies or young children. She'd be with other people in similar situations, women getting away from violent partners. The result is the clinic is very hot on security. But, most important, they offer counselling and support them after they leave, help them find a home, a job. And they have a vacancy coming up.'

She pressed her lips together, knew she was talking too much because she didn't want him to go. Her imagination went into overdrive—what if he got shot, like her father? But she knew he had to go, knew he would never send Stefan or any of his employees to face a danger he was unwilling to face himself.

'Isobel, it's going to be OK. I won't let Caro get hurt.'

'I'm not just worried about Caro. I'm worried about you.' The idea that something could happen to him weighted her limbs—fear he might get hurt, frustration that she couldn't go with him, the knowledge that life had no guarantees, could change irrevocably in a moment. Her mother's life, her own life had changed in the moment her father had made his fatal decision to get involved in a crime. 'Take care, OK? And I know it's not the time or place, but I do believe you. I believe that you didn't sleep with Anna.' She couldn't let him go into danger without telling him that.

'You don't have to say that.'

'I know. I'm saying it because I want you to know.' In truth, she wasn't even sure where the certainty came from, just knew that over the past days it had seemed increasingly impossible to believe that Jake would have behaved so dishonourably. A small voice in the back of her head questioned the wisdom of this leap of faith, pointed out that the evidence and the confession still stood. But Isobel dismissed them. Giving Jake the benefit of the doubt felt—right. Without hesitation, she stood on tiptoe and brushed her lips against his. Sensation shivered through her, a sweetness so potent she caught her breath. 'Good luck.'

His hand stroked her cheek and then, 'I'll see you later, I promise. And thank you for believing me. We'll talk later.'

Isobel watched him leave, knew the next few hours would be interminable and, despite her best efforts to remain busy and not give Emily bad vibes, that was exactly what those hours were. Minutes stretched and pulled as if time itself had morphed and slowed. Her thoughts jumbled and whirled as she wondered what was happening, whether everyone was safe, whether somehow Martin would prevail. Just as she'd always believed Simon could and would. Until finally her phone buzzed and she snatched it up, saw Jake's number.

'We're all safe. And on our way home.'

Isobel dropped the phone and picked Emily up for a cuddle. 'They did it,' she said. 'You are going to see your mummy.' Quickly, she raced to give Emily a bath, dressed her in her prettiest outfit, white with little pink flowers, and waited impatiently until she heard the front door open. She heard the pound of footsteps and then Caro tore into the room.

Isobel stepped forward to hand Emily over. Her friend looked tired but radiant as she smiled down at her daughter, even as tears glinted on her cheeks. 'I'm back, sweetheart. Mummy has missed you so much.' She looked up at Isobel. 'I was so scared, Isobel. So terrified I'd never see her again. Thank you. And I am so sorry. And it's so good to see you too.'

'And you Caro. Now, tell me what happened.' Isobel broke off as Jake entered the room, accompanied by a tall, lanky dark-haired man.

Caro blushed. 'This is Theo. He's my lawyer.

We were studying together before I dropped out and I went to him to help me with Martin. He was fabulous.'

'It was easy to be fabulous flanked by Jake and Stefan,' he said modestly and Isobel studied him. He had a kind face and eyes that also held a glint of humour—she liked him, she decided.

Jake grinned. 'We made a good team. Martin didn't know what hit him. Figuratively speaking,' he added.

Caro sat down, Emily still held close to her body.

'He was so...shocked; he couldn't believe I hadn't listened to him. He blustered a bit and made some threats but as soon as Jake stepped up to him he just deflated. Agreed to leave us alone, agreed he wouldn't come near Emily.' Worry touched her expression and she hugged Emily closer, lifted her to her shoulder. 'But I know he won't let us go that easy. I called the refuge and they sound incredible. I can move in in a few days.'

'And until then you can stay with me,' Isobel said firmly.

Caro shook her head. 'No. That's too dangerous. I'm going to stay at Theo's—Martin won't be able to find me there and Jake has assigned Stefan to stay with me until I get to the refuge.'

Isobel opened her mouth to argue and then she saw the glance Theo gave Caro; it held affection, kindness, strength and something else and she decided to hold her peace.

They spent the rest of the day catching up. Isobel and Caro sat in the garden and talked, rekindling a friendship that Isobel knew could never die completely. Until finally in the early evening Caro rose to her feet.

'Time to go. Thank you again, Isobel, and I won't ever lose touch with you again.' One final hug, a handshake with Theo and a final goodbye with Emily.

Isobel stood next to Jake on the driveway, waving until the car's tail-lights disappeared.

'It feels odd,' she said. 'I know we've only had Emily a few days but... I miss her. It's as though something is physically missing.'

'Our lives have revolved around Emily for the past few days—bottles, naptimes, nappies; it's amazing how quickly the human mind and body adapt.'

It was. It occurred to Isobel that it wasn't only Emily she'd got used to—it was Jake as well. Now it was time to move on and she was aware of a reluctance, a dip in her stomach, an unwillingness to say goodbye. How had that happened? Somehow he'd got under her skin and now she questioned whether the quest for closure had been a good one. In her head, she'd expected answers that would explain why Jake had betrayed her. Instead, all she had now was the belief that he hadn't, that she'd condemned him unjustly. Which opened up a vista of what-ifs and buts she didn't want to contemplate.

'It's natural to miss her,' Jake continued. 'But you should also be proud of yourself.'

'Proud?' She looked at him, a question in her eyes as he nodded emphatically.

'Yes. Caro is safe and with Emily and a lot of that is down to you as well as her.'

'And to you,' she said.

'We made a pretty good team.'

'We did.'

'But it's not over yet.'

Isobel looked at him. 'What do you mean?'

'It's like Caro said. I don't think that Martin will take this lying down. He was taken by surprise earlier and he knew he didn't stand a chance, but he was humiliated and he'll want revenge.'

'Then he'll go after Caro and Emily.' Panic caused the questions to emerge staccato. 'Will he be able to trace them? Does he have Theo's details?'

'Agreed and possibly and yes.' A tidal wave of fear rolled inside her, washing away her previous relief and pride, and Jake quickly took her hand in his. 'Whoa. It's OK. Theo and I came up with a plan. He isn't taking Caro and Emily back to his house—he's taking them to Wales, a farmhouse belonging to friends of his. There is no way Martin will find them there but, as an added precaution, Stefan has gone too.'

Relief touched her again and she squeezed his hand. 'Thank you. Again.'

'No thanks needed. It was Theo's idea and Stefan volunteered. He's very taken with Emily and he definitely did not like Martin.' Jake watched her for a moment. 'But that brings me to you.'

'Me?'

'Yes. If Martin can't find Caro or Theo he may turn his attention to you. And me. So I think we should stay here for a few more days. Give him a chance to cool down. What do you think?'

Isobel stared at him. What *did* she think? Conflicting thoughts jostled and head-butted each other in her brain. A part of her wanted to stay. Anticipation unfurled inside her at the thought of spending time with Jake, of exploring where they went from here, now they had closure. Another part told her that now they had closure there was nothing to discuss—the sensible option was to go.

CHAPTER NINE

JAKE TRIED TO focus on anything except Isobel's answer; he looked around the front garden at the vibrancy of the flowers in the early evening light, the deep green of the hedges, the hue of the sky. His shoulders tautened, his breath caught in his lungs and he forced himself to breathe properly. Realised that he wanted her to stay. Too much. Her face was scrunched in indecision and he decided, to hell with it. 'If you decide to go home I'll assign a security guard to you, but I'd like you to stay.'

'Why? I mean I'd like to stay but I don't know if it's a good idea.'

'Neither do I. But I'd still like you to stay.' He tried to gather his thoughts into coherence. 'If you stay maybe we can figure out if it's a good idea or not. If you go we'll never know.'

'That makes sense. I think.' Her face was still creased in indecision and he had the impression she was trying to both reassure and convince herself.

'Exactly,' he said. 'And things are different now—we need to talk about what you said earlier.' He hesitated. 'Did you mean it? Do you believe I told the truth about Anna?'

'Yes.' Her answer was unequivocal. 'I do believe you now. Six years ago I couldn't, because I was terrified I'd follow Mum's pattern. She allowed herself to believe Simon again and again. She believed his lies, believed he'd change, set herself up again and again. And I wished so much that the first time he hit her she'd walked out then.'

Jake reached out and placed a hand over hers. So much made sense now. 'I get that. Back then you thought you'd set a pattern for our relationship where I'd be unfaithful, lie, you'd believe me and I'd do it again.' And again and again. Just as Simon had abused her mother again and again.

Isobel nodded.

'I understand that.' He truly did, saw now how all her doubts and insecurities that he hadn't even known existed would have fed her belief that he could commit infidelity. Once confronted with a confession and the evidence, she couldn't let herself believe him; the risk had been too great. 'Thank you for believing me now.'

He realised he had a big smile on his face, not of triumph or vindication—more of happiness that she knew him to be innocent, that those hazel eyes no longer looked at him in judgement or doubt. But also because now Isobel knew that he hadn't cheated on her, that she hadn't been judged inferior to Anna, that he'd been happy with her.

Then he realised she wasn't smiling back, that worry still creased her brow.

'What's wrong?' he asked.

She shrugged. 'I messed up,' she said. 'If I'd believed you back then, what do you think would have happened to us?'

Jake inhaled a deep breath, watching a last flicker of sunlight highlight her chestnut hair with a pattern of blonde highlights. 'I think *I'd* have messed it up—I'm not cut out for a relationship. Work is too important to me; I don't think I could have balanced that with a relationship. And that wouldn't have been fair to you.'

'I haven't seen that side of you in the past few days,' she said.

'These past days have been an exception.' The lull before the boardroom storm—he'd done all the hard work in the past four years.

'This isn't who I really am.' A man who played with babies, fed the ducks, babysat at wedding rehearsals. 'My life is my work and I think that would have driven you away, would drive any woman away.' Soon enough he would be completely wedded to work, to implementing his plan. And he wanted that; the idea filled him with both excitement and anticipation.

And then it occurred to him that Isobel actually shared his work ethos, had an equal determination to succeed in her career. Could mutual ambition have worked for them rather than driven them apart? It wasn't a question he knew the answer to. 'But there's no point playing the what-if game.' He'd learnt that long ago too. You had to play the cards you were dealt, deal with the chips as they fell. 'This is where we are now and it's up to us where we go from here. Why don't you stay for the weekend and maybe we can figure that out?'

A long silence and then she nodded. 'OK. I'd like that.'

The smile broke out on his face again. 'Then I think we should go and celebrate. I've heard there's a great piano bar recently opened in Oxford, with amazing musicians and incredible cocktails as well. The clientele ranges from students to OAPs, a real mix.'

'It sounds perfect.' Her smile illuminated her

face, alleviated his realisation that he had no idea what he was doing. 'I'll go and change.' Yet as he watched her go a warning bell clamoured at the back of his brain, asked him whether this was a good idea. Events seemed to have overtaken him, their connection had crashed through the gears, evolved without his control or consent. Battened down emotions had escaped and right now Jake wasn't sure what to do about them.

Perhaps the answer was to think about work; he checked his messages and frowned at the sudden realisation he hadn't heard anything from the other board members for the past few days. And he hadn't contacted them either— had been so caught up in events that he hadn't given it much thought. That was a mistake and one he knew he needed to rectify. Quickly, he called his PA, left a message for her to call him back. He couldn't let the prize slip now, not when there was so much at stake.

The thoughts derailed as Isobel entered the room; his breath hitched in his throat as he absorbed her sheer beauty. Her chestnut hair fell in loose waves to frame her face, her hazel eyes were bright. She wore black jeans, topped by a strapless red vest top and a denim jacket.

'Let's go. I've ordered a taxi and it should be here—' his phone rang on cue '—right now.'

Minutes later they were en route to Oxford and Jake directed the driver to stop in the centre. Together they walked through the historic city. The shops were closed now but their displays still enticed. Further on, they walked past the facades of many of Oxford's most ancient buildings—the reason why it was dubbed the 'city of dreaming spires'—the Ashmolean Museum with its stunning architecture, the university colleges that had featured in so many blockbuster films, the oldest library in Europe and so very many literary places, pubs where authors had drunk.

'It's so strange, isn't it? To imagine Thomas Hardy sat in there,' Isobel said as they walked. 'He couldn't have known that so many years later people would still read his works. That people would study them.'

He nodded, suddenly aware that somehow they were hand in hand, her palm secure against his, and it felt—good. So he wasn't going to question it—after all, she'd told him she no longer believed Anna's confession, had absolved him. And tonight was about celebration of their teamwork.

'We turn down here,' he said.

'Have you been here before?' she asked and he shook his head.

'No. But someone told me about it and I was

thinking about maybe introducing the idea into the hotels. A piano bar, and maybe focus on cocktails.'

'So this is all about work,' she said, her tone tragic, and he turned to her with a startled look.

'No, I didn't mean it like that. I meant it came up in my research and I thought of it and—' He broke off as she grinned at him.

'Gotcha.' She squeezed his hand gently. 'I don't mind if it is about work. I'm happy to be your research partner. Lead me to the cocktails.'

They entered the dim interior of the low-ceilinged bar; brick walls showed posters of jazz greats and piano notes strummed the air, mixed with the buzz of conversation. A waiter approached, casually dressed in stone-washed jeans and a T-shirt imprinted with an image from one of the posters that decked the walls. 'I booked a table for two,' Jake said.

'Cool. This way.' He led them to a small round table tucked into an alcove, handed them both menus and left.

'Wow.' Isobel regarded the list. 'It may take me half the night to decide.'

He knew he should be focused on his own choice but he preferred to watch Isobel, the small cleft in her forehead as she studied the menu. 'You look as though the fate of the world hangs on your choice.'

'Ha ha! Not the fate of the world. But I don't drink often so I'd like to make sure I make the right choice. I can't decide whether I should play it safe or take a risk.'

Silence followed and an arrested look widened her hazel eyes before she quickly looked back down at the menu. The aftermath of her words rippled. Play it safe—keep their attraction contained? Or play with fire—flirt, banter, encourage the flames and hope they would dance to his tune?

The waiter returned and she gave a sigh that could indicate relief or regret. 'I'll play it safe. I'll have a Cosmopolitan, please. I know I like those.'

Jake looked at her and then back at the menu; he closed his eyes and jabbed a finger down. 'I'll have this one. Take a risk.'

The waiter nodded. 'Cool. They won't be long. Would you like to order food?'

Jake glanced down at the menu. 'I'll have the steak sandwich with fries.'

'Make that two,' Isobel said.

'Sure you don't want to try the katsu chicken burger with blue cheese? Take a risk?'

'I'm sure. And I can't afford to always take risks,' she said primly. 'I can't afford to discard my cocktail and just buy another if I don't like it.'

'I don't believe that had anything to do with your decision. And you don't either.' He grinned at her. 'In fact, admit it. You're annoyed you didn't take a risk.'

Her eyes narrowed, but he saw her lips quirk.

'Gotcha,' he said.

'OK, OK. But it will serve you right if you have ordered something revolting.'

The waiter arrived with their drinks and he looked at his doubtfully, noted the vivid blue colouring and the pineapple pieces.

'Looks good,' Isobel said, and she began to laugh, the low chuckle infectious, and he grinned at her.

'Want to go halves?' he offered.

'I'm good, thanks. With my nice safe Cosmopolitan.'

Jake sighed and sipped the vivid blue concoction. 'Actually, it's not that bad. I'm broadening my horizons.'

'Sure, sure.' She took another sip of hers and made an exaggerated sigh of appreciation. 'I think I'll stick with playing it safe.'

He held his glass up. 'To Caro and Emily.'

She clinked against his and smiled, thought for a moment. 'What did you think of Theo?'

'I liked him. He was calm under pressure and

he wasn't scared of Martin. I almost got the feeling he would have stood up to him without Stefan and me being there. I was chatting to him earlier, whilst you were with Caro, and he's definitely got a good head on his shoulders and he cares about Caro.' He watched her face, saw the conflict of expression. 'Didn't you like him?'

'I did. It's just… At the very start I liked Martin. And there is a theory that people follow patterns in life.' He watched as she traced a pattern on the table in a drop of liquid.

'You think Caro may be attracted to violent men?'

'Possibly, though I hope not.'

'Do you believe your life is following a pattern?'

Now she shrugged. 'It's hard to know, isn't it? I do know that a lot of children who suffer domestic violence can go on to abuse others. I *know* I won't do that. I couldn't imagine ever hurting someone else, let alone a child. I also know, though, that sadly often women do go from one abusive relationship to another. I believe that your past shapes you and you can't undo that.'

Jake shook his head. 'I disagree. Your past is part of you but it doesn't have to shape you. You shape yourself, control your own destiny.'

'To a point, of course you do. We all have choices but I'm not sure how free those choices are. Maybe you don't want children because of what happened to you as a baby.'

'No.' His denial was vehement. 'I don't want children because I recognise I couldn't give them a family life they'd deserve.' Yet even he could sense that his tone was over-emphatic.

Now she raised her eyebrows. 'But perhaps you couldn't give them a family life because you didn't experience one. Maybe the same goes for me.'

He considered the idea for a moment. 'So you're saying if we both had experienced conventional childhoods, with two happy parents, a pet and a picket fence we'd want to repeat the pattern ourselves.'

'Yes. And a bit of me is sad that I don't think I can do it. When I think of Emily a part of me does want a baby of my own. Surely you felt the same way? I saw you with her—you bonded, you were a natural.'

The question jolted him, projecting a sudden image of himself looking down at his own baby, a tiny being with chestnut hair and hazel eyes. The sheer idea pierced him with a strange emotion, gave rise to a debate he didn't want to have—did he actually want a child, despite acknowledging the impossibility of fatherhood? For a moment a sense of discomfort probed at the decision he had made long ago—that Cartwright came first, that it would be irresponsible to have a baby when he had no wish to commit to a relationship, when he knew that relationships had no guarantee.

The thought of Cartwright steadied him—that was his future, his legacy. His decision was correct and he refused to be saddened by it. He shook his head. 'I'm good with my life choices. That's the important thing. To have no regrets.' Yet despite the clarity of his words the image of that baby still lingered and he met Isobel's gaze. 'That's why, if you have regrets about your choice, don't be afraid to change your mind. I can only imagine how difficult your childhood was but I don't believe that means you can't be a brilliant parent yourself. In fact I know you would be.'

'Thank you.' He heard the sincerity in her words but suspected she didn't believe him. 'So would you. I hope you believe that.' Her hazel eyes studied him with way too much discernment and to his own annoyance his gaze dropped to his nearly finished drink, studied the final piece of pineapple. In truth, he didn't believe that at all; he knew he would never abandon a child or treat them with indifference but he knew he would be unable to balance his love for his job with the needs of a child. And he would not contemplate being an absentee parent—that would make him no better than his own father. Neither would he take his child to work—would never place a mantle of expectation on them, make them believe all he wanted was a successor—that would make him no better than his grandfather.

Isobel reached out, placing a hand over his. 'Listen to me,' she said. 'I get it's hard for either of us to believe we could be good parents, but I think there's something we should both remember. We did a fabulous job over the past few days with Emily.' Now she smiled. 'And we're meant to be celebrating!' She raised her glass and they both drank the final gulp of their drinks.

'One more?' he asked.

'Just the one. Hopefully, the food will absorb the alcohol and we haven't really had a chance to listen to the music. It would be great to sit here for a little longer and soak it in.'

'What would you like?'

Now she smiled at him, a huge sunny smile. 'I'll have the seventh one on the second page. Whatever it is.' She paused. 'As long as it isn't your blue one!' Another smile. 'I'll take the risk.'

He grinned back. 'You've got it.'

As he approached the bar his phone buzzed—his PA, returning his call of earlier. Quickly he put the phone to his ear. 'Hi, Bethany.'

CHAPTER TEN

ISOBEL LOOKED UP as Jake returned and handed her a vivid orange drink. A Mai Tai,' he said, and smiled. 'Rum, pineapple juice and almond liqueur.'

But his smile was edged with preoccupation and she frowned. 'You OK?'

'Fine.'

Doubts suddenly assailed her. 'Look, if you don't want me to stay, I don't have to.'

He held up a hand. 'It's not that. At all. I do want you to stay. I got a call—a work-related one, that's all.'

'Bad news?'

'Not exactly. More a bit of a wake-up call. I have an important board meeting next week and I need to do some work.'

'That's fine—really. I get work is important.' Yet irrational disappointment surfaced that this weekend would be impinged on. 'Truly I don't mind going home tomorrow morning. Or—'

'There is no need for you to go home. In fact I was wondering if you'd like to go to a ball tomorrow night? The work I had in mind is networking.'

'A ball?'

'Yes. It's a charity gala bash, held annually in London at the Milton Park Hotel. The guests will be a mixture of businessmen and celebrities. Cartwright usually takes a table and I and some of the other board members attend. I'd planned to go, but I cancelled as I thought we'd be with Emily. But now I could go and it would give me a chance to chat with the other board members.'

Isobel shook her head. 'That's really not my sort of thing.' Understatement of the year— the thought of mingling with high-flying executives and celebrities at a star-studded event made anxiety flutter her nerves into agitation. The thought of going with Jake sent the panic into the stratosphere. 'It's not my style.'

He shook his head, his grey eyes glittering with bemusement. 'I don't get it. You organise events like this charity gala.'

'Exactly. I'm an organiser; it gives me status, a reason to be there. I'm not being judged for myself but for the job I do and I don't have a problem with that. I'm good at what I do.'

'You're also good at being you. You would easily hold your own in a crowd like that.'

Isobel shook her head, wondering how to make him understand. 'Not in that context. I wouldn't know what to say or how to behave, or what to wear or—'

Jake sipped his drink, studying her for a moment. 'How about we do it this way? You think about it as work, come in your professional capacity. Come to network. The place will be full of people who could help promote your business, people who use events companies a lot.' He leant back and smiled at her, a smile that curled her toes and spoke of his satisfaction at finding an argument he knew to be unassailable.

A smile he was entitled to—he had her. Clara would be thrilled and Isobel knew this was too big an opportunity to be missed. If she could get even a single contact it would be gold.

'You in?' he asked.

'I'm in.'

'Then it's a date.'

The simple phrase rolled through the air as if carried by the notes of the piano, changing the tempo of the evening. A date with Jake? The idea sent a funny little thrill through her veins. 'Is it?' she asked before she could stop herself.

'Do you want it to be?' he countered.

Isobel looked down at her drink, took a small sip on the brightly coloured straw. The tang of pineapple contrasted with the hint of almond, the overall effect both refreshing and a hint sinful because of the kick from the rum. His question whirled in her head: did she want it to be a date? To risk a cocktail choice was one thing—to hazard a date was a whole new strata of jeopardy. She made her decision.

'No. This ball is about work—you said you need to talk to the board and I want to try and network to make contacts. So let's not blur those lines.'

'Fair enough. But I want you to know that I'd be proud to take you as my date. You are courageous and intelligent and professional and loyal. And beautiful and poised and graceful.'

The sincerity in his voice touched her; she knew he believed the words even if she couldn't.

'Got it?' he asked.

'Got it,' she replied, mesmerised by his voice, his gaze, the way he was looking at her.

'And you will wow every single one of those guests tomorrow night.'

'OK.' Now she did smile. 'If you're ever out of a job you could have a whole new career as a coach. You give a mean pep talk.'

'Thank you.'

She glanced at him, aware of a daft shyness. 'You really think I'm all those things?'

'I really do.' Now his voice was husky. 'I meant every word. I want you to be able to see it—to see yourself like I see you. The ugliness of your childhood isn't you; you're like a beam of light that shines through it.'

The beauty of his words overwhelmed her and she leant forward and oh, so gently brushed his lips with her own, tasting the fruit juice, the slight tang of alcohol. She raised her hand to his cheek, lingered on the roughness of his six o'clock shadow, closed her eyes and let the strains of the music envelop her.

Hearing his small groan, she threw caution to the wind. She simply lost herself in the moment, in the kiss, in the soaring sensations he aroused in her, in the gentleness and the depth of passion, unsure what this meant, whether it was a symbol of closure or a way of showing her gratitude for his words.

The change of song as the pianist morphed into something more rock 'n' roll pulled her out of the spell and she sat back, stared at him. 'No regrets,' she said instantly. The feeling liberated her. She had no idea where this weekend would take them, but she'd wanted that kiss. A kiss, now she knew he wasn't a philanderer, wasn't a liar, hadn't betrayed her. She'd deserved one guilt-free kiss. And it had been a humdinger.

'No regrets,' he echoed.

For a moment the urge to kiss him again threatened but that, she knew, would be a mistake. Time for practicalities.

'So what time will we need to leave tomorrow? Because I need to go shopping.'

'That's fine. We'll get a train up to London in the afternoon, stop at mine to change and then Roberto can drive us to the event. Then we can either stay in London or come back here.'

'Come back here.' The words left her lips without hesitation; she knew she didn't want to stay in a fancy hotel, she wanted this weekend to be spent in the cottage where they had shared so much and found closure.

'Then we'll head into Oxford in the morning, shop and we could visit the cathedral if you like?'

'It's a plan.'

CHAPTER ELEVEN

THE FOLLOWING MORNING Isobel stood in the changing room of a small boutique in the centre of Oxford and looked at the two dresses hanging on the peg in front of her.

Two dresses. One choice.

The two were completely different—both were professional, but there it ended. Dress number one was demure, black, fitted, high neckline, it contoured her body and wearing it she looked svelte and elegant. She'd look good, but she wouldn't stand out. It was the play it safe dress...

Then there was dress number two, which was more shadowy, more shimmery—a dress that skirted with danger. Nude underlay with a chiffon overlay patterned with a black flower and leaf pattern, a V-necked front that tantalised without revelation, and then the material shimmered to the floor in a waterfall of perfect folds. But it was what the dress lacked that made it stand out—in short, it left her back bare.

Isobel had never worn anything like it, but it made her feel—different. Sexy, alluring—perhaps the likes of Anna and Julia always felt like this. The idea was a strange one. And she wanted Jake to see her in this, wanted to knock his socks off, wanted to live up to his words.

Beautiful, poised and graceful.

She wanted to add to that list. Even if she sensed the dress represented danger, a skirmish with risk.

She stared at the dresses. Two dresses. One choice.

Jake stood outside the cathedral, spotting Isobel with unerring accuracy as she threaded her way through the twisty, windy streets that spoke of so much history, watched the grace of her movement, the sway of her chestnut hair in the breeze.

As she approached, he smiled at her. 'Successful shop?'

'Yes.' The word was said with emphasis and he raised an eyebrow.

'Good.' He looked at her, hoping that last night he'd made her see herself as she truly was. For a moment their kiss haunted him; it had held an intensity he couldn't explain, it had avowed something. Dammit. Forget the kiss—his focus needed to be on his meeting with the board members later on. Bethany had reported that in the few days of his absence Charles Cartwright had actually been seen in the office, had met with the other board members individually. It was possible that his father was going to try and make a fight of it.

'Shall we go in?'

She looked up at the exterior. 'I thought it would be bigger.'

'It's one of the smallest cathedrals in England, but it's like a slice of history.'

They entered and next to him Isobel gave a small gasp of wonder as she took in the rich vaulted ceiling in its splendour, the glory of the stained-glass windows.

'It's awe-inspiring.'

'So is the story behind it,' he said. 'Originally this was a church that grew up around the shrine of a saint—a woman called Frideswide. She was an important noblewoman who founded a priory in Oxford. But she caught the eye of a Mercian king who didn't care about her vows of celibacy—he wanted to marry her anyway. She fled, he chased her and was struck down. Frideswide went on to live to a ripe old age as an abbess in a nunnery; she is also said to have created a well with healing powers. She died in about 750 AD.'

Isobel gave a small shiver. 'And we're still talking about her nearly ten centuries after her death. And she might have stood here on this very spot at some point in her life. The idea is so…immense.'

It was the perfect word and again he felt that sense of connection, of being attuned with her as they continued through the cathedral and entered the chapel.

Isobel paused to read the memorials. 'So many Cavaliers were buried here as well. All those men who believed in their king and ended up dead.'

'Soldiers who fought bravely for an ideal, those who believed it was Charles I's right, his divine destiny to be King.' Destiny—those soldiers had fought and lost their lives to protect the destiny of one man. Had it been choice or simply fear of the repercussions if they didn't? Or a simple need to earn money? He recalled Isobel's assertion of the previous evening—that people had choices but they weren't always as free as you might believe they were. What about his own choices? His choice to wrest control of Cartwright. His destiny or his choice? 'And then the Roundheads, who believed no one should be given that right just because of their birthright. They fought equally as bravely and their victory in the end was short-lived.'

'But their actions had huge repercussions,' she said. 'Future monarchs had less power and then still less and eventually they lost the power to rule. Yet their destiny is still to be royal.' There was little choice to be had there.

They stood for a moment and then she looked up at him. 'I get the feeling this place is important to you.'

'It is.' He met her gaze squarely, knowing he wanted to share this with her, in the same way she had shared with him the previous day. 'I came here soon after I met my mother.'

'When you were eighteen, you said?'

'Yes, I went to find her when I was eighteen. I wanted some answers. Until then I'd always bottled it; at eighteen it seemed the right time. I traced her to California, arrived unannounced. She was...shocked.' At the time he'd been unable to figure if that shock had been born of sadness or horror or happiness. Perhaps a mixture of them all. 'But she explained why she'd left. Explained it all. It turned out that my grandfather delivered my father with an ultimatum. Told him if he didn't get married and produce an heir he would disown him. My father obeyed the letter of the law—he paid my mother to marry him and produce a child. She agreed because she was desperate. Her younger brother needed an operation, one he could only get in America if someone paid for it. My dad offered to do that. In return my mother had to give me up. So that's what she did. To save her brother. My dad gave me up so that he could save his lifestyle. My grandfather instigated my birth in order to mould an heir.'

Her hazel eyes were wide, full of compassion. 'I cannot believe any of them acted like that, without any thought for you. And you, at eighteen, if you didn't know any of this it must have been a cataclysmic shock.'

It had been exactly that—the facts had torpedoed his beliefs. Until then he'd believed his grandfather had stepped in out of love; now he realised that in fact his grandfather had orchestrated his creation—had demanded an heir and been presented with one. It hadn't been love; it had been a man's desire to live on through his legacy.

'That's what I came here to think about,' he said. 'My mother's explanation at least gave me clarity, explained the way they'd behaved. At least my mother had some excuse; as for my father, I have always known how important his lifestyle is to him. The real whammy was my grandfather—I knew he had always wanted me to be the Cartwright heir but I had always believed he took me in out of love. I wanted to do as he wished because I loved him too and I felt I owed it to him.' He shrugged. 'But once I knew the truth I realised I owed him nothing.'

She had moved close to him now. 'You must have had so much to think about; it must have made you question your whole life.'

He nodded. 'I could renounce my inheritance, build my own empire, I could become a doctor or a blacksmith. And I looked at all these people here.' He gestured to the gravestones. It made me think about the decisions they made. St Frideswide—maybe she didn't even want to become a nun, maybe her parents decided that for her. Maybe it tore families apart when some declared for the king and others for Cromwell. I thought about my grandfather and I realised that I wanted to lead Cartwright, not because it was my destiny but because it was what I wanted to do.' He'd known that he couldn't abandon the business; to him the empire was too real, almost like a live entity.

'Have you ever regretted it?'

'Not once.'

'What about today? Have you come here today to make a decision?' she asked.

Had he? It was an astute question. Had he

come here to question his current course—a course that set him on a collision path with his father. A fight for control of the board. A fight he would win—he'd put the work in, proved his worth and now it was time for his vision to take the company forward. The decision had been made and there was no way he'd back down now. He hadn't come here to decide but to seek some sort of validation.

Perhaps men had come here in previous centuries to decide where their allegiances lay— come to ask for advice or guidance, hoping that St Frideswide would guide them on the righteous path. In the here and now he knew he had no choice—he needed to wrest power or watch the business stagnate and crumble and he wouldn't—couldn't do that. Charles Cartwright had opposed Jake's every effort to take Cartwright into the future. Jake believed that his father was worried that the new plan was too risky, might jeopardise his income stream and lifestyle. He didn't trust Jake to take the helm. In which case, now was the time to be ruthless, to continue his efforts to unseat the man who had never wanted him in the first place.

'My decision is already made,' he said and glanced at his watch. 'Now, we need to get back. We have a ball to prepare for.' He was looking forward to it, though a small niggle accosted him, a worry that somehow his father had undermined him, somehow turned the other members. Hell, it would only take one of the others to vote against Jake and with Charles—and Jake would lose.

A few hours later they arrived at his home, a terraced three-bedroom house that his grandfather had left him. He had let it out until he'd inherited his shares and decided it would be sensible to have a base in London. He saw Isobel glance around, tried to see how his home must look through her eyes. The décor was neutral, cool greys and stone colours, the furniture chosen for comfort and ease.

'I like it,' Isobel said and he felt a sense of pleasure at her approval.

'You can change in the spare room,' he said. 'It has an en suite bathroom—if there is anything you need, just shout. I'll be through there.' He pointed down the hallway to his room.

Isobel nodded. 'Thank you. I'll try not to be too long.'

'No problem. Roberto is picking us up at seven so we've got plenty of time.'

Enough that he settled down to do some work before quickly showering and donning his tux. He exited the room and made his way to the lounge. 'Ready to…' The words died on his lips, his brain froze as he halted and simply stared at Isobel. 'I… You…' There simply weren't words for how she looked—the dictionary didn't cover it. The best he could do was, 'You look stunning.' The dress could have been made for her, the bold black pattern eye-catching, the material moulded to her figure and swept in regal folds to the floor. Her hairstyle was simple, falling to her shoulders in sleek chestnut waves, her make-up discreet, yet it emphasised the hazel of her eyes and the generous curve of her lips. Political correctness be damned, he couldn't take his eyes off her, couldn't help but let his eyes rove her body.

'Thank you. I wanted to live up to the occasion.' Her hazel eyes sparkled and her cheeks flushed slightly.

'Truly, you look sensational.' He gestured towards the door. 'The car awaits.' Isobel walked past him and now Jake nearly swallowed his tongue as he clocked her bare back, smooth creamy skin, her slender waist accentuated by the cut of the dress, and he closed his eyes. Heaven help him.

Roberto climbed out of the car to open the back door and they slid onto the smooth leather seats. 'Well, I'm quite happy to sit here and look at you for the whole journey,' he said.

'You don't scrub up so badly yourself.'

She smiled but as the car ate up the miles he could sense a proportionate growth in the tension in her body, saw her hands clench. 'You don't need to be nervous.'

'I'm not nervous. I'm bricking it.' She closed her eyes. 'Oh, God. What if I say something like that to someone important?'

'You won't—and it wouldn't matter if you did. You will fit in, Iz. And you look incredible.'

'Yes, but I've realised that doesn't make any difference. I used to try to dress the part as a child. It wasn't easy but sometimes Mum and I would manage a shopping day out, buy new clothes, and I'd try to wear what the popular girls wore. I'd go into school and hope, really hope they would include me. But they never did. They knew where I came from, knew I was the weird kid.' He could hear the bitter-tinged resignation in her voice. 'People can tell and they will be able to tell now, that I don't fit.' Her foot tapped the floor. 'Who did you take last year?'

'Hayley Jensen.'

'The supermodel?' Her voice was tauter than a fixed crossbow and Jake knew that words wouldn't cut it, knew that nothing he said would take away her gut belief that she was still the weird kid, about to be ridiculed by celebrities and executives alike. 'Turn round,' he instructed.

'Why?'

'You'll see. Nothing sinister, I promise.'

She did as he asked and he inhaled silently, looking at the bare skin of her back, the curve of her shoulder blades.

Then carefully he lifted his hands, brushing her hair out of the way, feeling a shiver ripple across her skin. He began to massage her shoulders, felt the tautness, the knots and realised exactly how tense she was. Gently he kneaded and worked, heard her small moan as he began to dissolve the tightness.

'That's amazing,' she murmured when he decided that any more would be too much. For her and for him. The urge to kiss the nape of her neck, to turn her round and capture her lips was almost too strong to withstand. 'Thank you.'

'You're welcome.' His attempt to keep his voice even was a spectacular fail and he cleared his throat. 'I hope it helped.'

'It did, thank you.' Her breathing had quickened slightly, heat tinged her cheekbones and he knew she was as affected as he was.

This had to stop; he needed to focus. This ball was about work. He couldn't afford the slightest risk to his plans—plans he had made over the past four years. His mission was so nearly achieved—he couldn't let himself be distracted.

'Good. Now, I just need to get a bit of work done, if that's OK.'

'Me too,' she said and he saw his own guilt mirrored on her expression. 'I've got a list of people I should try and approach,' she explained. 'And a few facts about them. I need to make sure I've memorised them.'

CHAPTER TWELVE

ISOBEL SMILED AT Roberto as he opened the door for her and she climbed out, felt the welcome evening breeze on her face. Welcome because she'd got herself all hot and bothered or, rather, Jake had. Her skin still tingled from the brand of his hands, the slow sensuous massage imprinted as his fingers had wielded their magic, ratcheted up her body's need for him.

Whoa.

Not need. She didn't need him; she would never need anyone. Never give that power. Now his hand touched the small of her back and she nearly yelped. She forced herself to focus on their destination, the lavish exterior of the Milton Park Hotel, lit up now by an array of twinkling lights that shone on a deep red carpet, upon which milled an assortment of celebrities and a stream of photographers and TV crew. Cameras abounded and Isobel blinked at how utterly surreal it was for her to be here.

Oh, God, what was she doing here? Her eyes widened as she recognised people hitherto only seen on TV or glimpsed on the covers of celebrity gossip magazines At least no one would want to take a picture of her. And now, as she looked at the dresses of the other guests, doubts hustled her.

Then Jake took her hand. 'Walk tall,' he whispered. 'You deserve to be here.'

The feel of his hand steadied her and she glanced up at him with a quick grateful smile. Just as, from nowhere, there was a cry of, 'Jakey!' and a tall blonde woman glided into their path.

Hayley Jensen. Of course it was. Isobel looked up at the stunning model and felt herself pale into insignificance.

'Hayley.'

'Jakey! I hoped you'd be here. I want you to meet Matt.' The slender blonde waved her left hand at them. 'We're engaged! Matt's a surgeon. Let's get a picture.' Hayley waved and almost immediately she and her fiancé were surrounded by photographers.

Before even a stray reporter could home in on them, Jake moved towards the hotel entrance and they entered the lobby, ushered in by the magnificent moustached porter stood at the revolving door.

Once inside, they were asked to sign the guest register and after a discreet security check they entered the ballroom, which glittered from the lights of four ornate chandeliers that dipped from the high vaulted ceilings. Round tables were beautifully decorated with white and pink floral centrepieces and matching helium balloons floated above silver champagne buckets. Isobel forced herself not to shrink backwards, stayed close to Jake as a silver-haired man made his way through the throng towards them. 'Jake! Glad you could make it.'

'Good to see you, Dillon. This is Isobel, an old friend of mine. Isobel this is Dillon, a board member at Cartwright.'

'Rumour had it you wouldn't be here.' Dillon's eyes narrowed. 'Especially as you've missed a couple of meetings recently.'

'Yes. It was unavoidable, I'm afraid.'

'Hmm. Not the best timing. Clarissa and I were wondering if you'd bottled it. Or simply changed your mind. As your father says, you're still young, maybe you'd rather have a more relaxed lifestyle.' Now his gaze went to Isobel and she knew that he believed her to be part of the relaxation package.

Isobel felt Jake tense beside her, saw his jaw clench. 'I'm sure my father would prefer it if I did exactly that,' he said smoothly. 'However, that is not my intention. I'm sorry that I've been away from the office for a few days. I agree that it was unfortunate timing, but I'm around now and happy to go over any points you would like to discuss. Either this evening or any time that's convenient to you.'

The man looked mollified. 'Good, I know that Angela and Jonathan have a few doubts as well. They are here too. And Clarissa. Perhaps we could all have a chat. You're asking us to put our faith in you.'

'I know that, but I'm confident that my plan is the right way forward and that I can allay your concerns. In fact I'd welcome the chance—I want us to be agreed on this.'

'I'll go and tell the others you're here and up for a talk.'

Isobel watched as Dillon walked away.

'Everything OK?'

'It will be.' Now his tension was palpable. 'It's my fault—I should have kept better tabs on them the past few days, seen them in person.'

'Has looking after Emily affected your work in some way?'

'No.' He shook his head. 'It's nothing to do with Emily. I just made a small miscalculation, took my eye off the ball. I'll sort it out.'

But there was a trace of frustration in his voice, the tiniest hint of worry, and Isobel shook her head, knowing it wouldn't help if Dillon believed Jake had been on a short and sweet romance with her.

She glanced round the seething mass of people and took a deep breath, tugging her hand from Jake's. 'I'll be right back. Nature calls.'

But, as she left him, her eyes scanned the room for Dillon, finally pinpointed him in conversation with three others, no doubt the other board members. Isobel cleaved a way through the crowd towards them.

'Hi,' she said.

Dillon looked round. 'Hi—Isobel, was it?'

'Yes, I'm Jake's friend and as his friend I wanted to clear something up with you. The past days—Jake's absence—he has been helping a friend of ours and what he's done has genuinely changed a child's life.'

Dillon frowned. 'Jake's whereabouts are his business—he doesn't have to explain it to us.'

'He isn't,' the red-haired woman pointed out, 'this young lady is. Please go on, Isobel. I'm Clarissa, by the way.'

'Earlier, I got the impression that you believe that Jake was spending his time on holiday. He wasn't. A mutual friend of ours is a subject of domestic abuse; Jake stepped in to help look after her baby and help her. I am quite sure that you want to be led by a man with principles. I wanted you to know that Jake has those.'

Clarissa nodded. 'Thank you, Isobel,' she said. 'I doubt Jake would have shared that with us. And it is worth taking into account.' As she turned away, Isobel heard her say, 'It seems as though Charles was wrong in his assessment of the situation.'

As she headed back through the crowd Jake approached her. 'Is everything Ok?'

'Yes.' Isobel hesitated, then decided it would be better to tell Jake the truth—he needed to know the exact score. 'I spoke to Dillon to explain that you haven't been skiving off the past days, that you've been doing something good.'

His gaze softened as he stared into her eyes and her insides started to go gooey. 'You didn't have to go to bat for me.'

'Yes, I did. I don't know exactly what is going on but I know how much Cartwright means to you. My assumption is you need their support for something important.'

His hand came up and he gently brushed a strand of hair off her face, the gesture so soft, so gentle, so sensual that she closed her eyes.

'So now you go and talk to them. I'll be fine.'

'I'm not going to abandon you.'

'You aren't. I'm here to network.' She tried to keep the wobble from her voice, knew damn well she was going to go and hide in the toilet rather than introduce herself to anyone.

'Nope.' Jake glanced around and, before she could stop him, he waved at Hayley.

'No, I don't want—'

'She's a nice person, Isobel, and she and I were never an item. Truly.'

Before she could speak, Hayley had reached them. 'Hayley, could you help me out? Isobel here is an events planner and a damned good one. I was hoping to introduce her to a few people but—'

'Don't tell me, work calls.' Hayley shook her head. 'This is just what he was like last year,' she said. 'I barely saw him—he was so busy working.'

'Go.' Isobel made a shooing gesture and after a second's hesitation Jake turned and headed towards the board members.

Isobel smiled weakly at Hayley. 'Look, you don't have to babysit me. I know there are plenty of other things you'd rather be doing and—'

'Nope, I'm more than happy to help. I only come to these things because it's for a good cause and my agent tells me to. Parties aren't really my thing.'

'Oh.'

Hayley watched Jake for another moment. 'It's probably the last we'll see of him,' she prophesied. 'One of the many reasons why he and I could never have worked. But he's a nice guy. Upfront, you know?' She took a couple of glasses of champagne from a passing waiter and passed one to Isobel. 'We figured on our first date that we were not going to work. I want the real thing—love, kids, a farm in the countryside. I love modelling, for sure, but I'll be happy to retire in a few years. I've invested my money well and I want to settle down and have loads of children. And chickens.'

'Chickens?'

'Yup. And a horse and dogs—and Matt wants that too. And I'll live in wellies and old clothes and no make-up.'

Isobel blinked—this was not how she'd pictured the conversation going.

'Anyway, let's start introducing you.'

Her nerves still strummed but Hayley's easy confidence, the knowledge that underneath the glamour the model wanted nothing more than to muck out pigs whilst dressed in wellies imbued Isobel with a strange confidence.

And, to her surprise, most of the people Hayley introduced her to were easy to talk to; the ability to hide behind a professional per-

sona was a huge help and soon Isobel relaxed
and the next hour glided past until she sensed
rather than saw Jake approach.

'How's it going?' He came up beside her,
where she was standing watching the dance
floor being set up, a glass of juice in her hand.
'I'm sorry I was so long.'

'It's truly fine. Hayley was great—she wants
us to plan her engagement party—I've made
some really good contacts and I have a whole
list of follow-ups and a couple of meetings.
Clara is going to go ballistic with joy. How
did it go for you?'

Jake exhaled. 'Good. I'll make sure I stay on
them until next week but I think they're back
on board, pardon the pun. Thank you for what
you did. It was kind.'

'I told the truth.' She'd known that Jake
wouldn't have wanted to sound as though he
were making excuses.

He looked to where the orchestra were preparing to start.

'It was still kind and it made a difference.
May I have the honour of the first dance?'

The seriousness of his voice made her skin
shiver in anticipation, as if it were in truth an
honour. It's a dance, she told herself. No big
deal. But her body wasn't buying that. Because
she'd be in his arms, up close and personal,

and that was a massive deal. Even if she wasn't sure of the terms.

'You may,' she said softly and it felt as though she were committing to something far more.

Just a dance, she tried again.

He took her hand, the grasp so firm and right, and he led her onto the floor, where the orchestra had started to play. One arm encircled her waist and now his hand was on her bare back and his touch felt decadent, glorious, like a brand, and she knew that it would be impossible for her to dance with anyone else. The thought of another hand on her felt wrong.

And this felt so right; her body seemed made for his. She pressed against him with a small sigh of relief, her cheek against the solid breadth of his chest, her hand on the muscular strength of his shoulder. She swayed with him to the music, lost in a world of pure sensation—the lilting, melodic notes that touched and wove through the air, the soft cloth of his tuxedo, the muffled beat of his heart, the scent of his soap, the feel of the skin on the nape of his neck against her fingers—his small gasp when she placed her fingers there. And then the tune danced its way to a close.

'And now for something a little more lively, ladies and gents. Are you ready now?'

She stepped back as the music morphed into a faster beat, the drums and the trumpets mixed it up and jolted her out of her near trancelike state.

'You up for this?' he asked and she nodded, hoped that the segue from slow and romantic to this would shake the dreamy languor from her mind and body.

And it did—but now her whole body pulsed to a different type of dream; this was about passion and movement and as he twirled her away from him and then back hard and fast into the strength of his body, desire changed its tempo from languor to sharp and edgy and needy. Until the final notes and then he caught her, laughing and breathless and wanting, yearning him.

'You didn't tell me you were such an expert,' he said, but she could sense the words were an attempt to impose normality. Because his grey eyes had darkened with desire, his body told her that his need matched hers, that the same burn of longing lashed his body too.

'I'm not. It's you.' Their bodies were attuned on the dance floor, as they had been in the bedroom, a reminder she so did not need right now. She knew she should step back, from their proximity, from the rush that cascaded her body, from the signals that threatened to overload her brain, which was telling her the desire had to be doused. Her biggest problem now was that she no longer remembered why. 'Just you.' Now she knew that no level of argument, of logic, could stem this. And she no longer wanted to. If it was a bad idea so be it; she'd take the consequences. 'Jake?'

'Yes?' His deep voice was low with desire.

'I… When this is over, I want… I want… you.'

Just him.

'Are you sure?'

'Yes. What do you think?' She stared now at the buttons on his tux, focused on the material until she felt dizzy.

Then, 'Look at me.'

She did. 'I don't think, I *know* that I want you. So much it hurts.'

Afterwards, Isobel had no idea how she got through the rest of the ball, knew she must have, hoped she managed it with professional courtesy and calm. Knew she must have eaten, knew too that the food must have been gorgeously, meltingly good. But all she could think about was the night ahead. Then finally, eventually they had said their goodbyes and were heading for the car. He slid in after her and took her hand, held it in a cool firm grasp, his thumb circling her palm. The rhythm, the movement was poignantly sensual and desire built, burned inside her as the car ate up the miles until finally, finally they were back at the cottage.

A farewell to Roberto, who was driving back to London, and then they half ran up the pathway to the front door. The keys—why was it taking so long?—his fingers made clumsy by a need for haste. Then he swung the door open and they bundled in, laughing as they nearly got stuck in the doorway.

'I can't slow down,' she said. 'I want you so very badly.'

He swept her up into his arms and headed for the stairs, then straight up and into his bedroom, where he placed her gently down so she faced him. 'Here I am. However you want me.'

Now she smiled and it was a slow languorous smile as if now they were finally at this point she could slow down, take her time. 'Naked would be a good start.'

'That can be arranged.'

'Allow me.' She stepped forward and her fingers deftly undid the buttons of his shirt; she placed her hand on his chest and she could feel his heartbeat accelerate under her fingers.

'I lied earlier,' she said. 'I didn't buy this dress for the occasion; I bought it for you. Just you.'

'For my eyes only.' Another pulse of desire jolted through her and he gently turned her round, dropped the lightest of kisses on the nape of her neck, trailed his fingers over her bare back and the shiver of her response shuddered her body. Deftly he unhooked the dress and she felt the silky folds slither down and pool on the floor. She heard his groan and then she turned round, stepped forward into his arms and they tumbled backwards onto the bed.

CHAPTER THIRTEEN

ISOBEL OPENED HER EYES, aware of a dreamy, wonderful sense of joy, happiness, release… Memories of the past hours tumbled over her and she turned to look at Jake, who still lay asleep, one arm flung over her in a protective embrace.

The glorious realisation that she was allowed to study him filled her with a warm gooey sense of happiness—the nape of his neck, the breadth of his bare back, the tangle of the duvet round their legs all brought a goofy smile to her face. Unable to help herself, still amazed that she could, she gently trailed her fingers down his back and he rolled over and smiled a big lazy grin.

'Morning.'

'Morning.'

He shifted so that she could snuggle into the crook of his arm. 'Sleep well?' he asked.

'Yup. I feel incredibly refreshed and—' Her

tummy gave a small rumble. 'And incredibly hungry.'

'I'll rustle us up some breakfast. Stay right where you are. I'll be back with breakfast in bed.'

'You are…amazing,' she said. 'In more ways than one,' she added as she watched him climb out of bed, completely unselfconscious in his nakedness. He pulled on a pair of jeans and a T-shirt and smiled down at her. 'Hold that thought,' he said.

Once he had left the room Isobel scrambled out of bed and used the bathroom, glanced around the room in search of clothing and oh, so daring, pulled open a drawer and took out one of Jake's T-shirts. She pulled it over her head and revelled in the feel of it, the smell of it; the sheer intimacy of wearing his clothes sent her giddy.

Slow down, Isobel.

An inner voice tried to insert a word of caution and she shut it down. Consequences be damned; whatever happened, the next days would be conducted without analysis or regret.

Jake entered carrying a laden tray and brought it over to the chest of drawers. 'Help yourself.'

'Where did you get these from?'

'I made a quick run down to the local bakery.'

Pastries, toast, butter, scones, jam... Isobel heaped her plate and carried it back to the bed and soon they were sitting cross-legged, facing each other and eating with gusto.

'This is perfect,' she said. Before he could respond his phone rang. Placing his plate down, he reached for it, glanced at the number and then rose lithely to his feet and put the phone to his ear.

'Good morning, Clarissa.' He listened for a minute and then smiled. 'That's great to hear and thank you. Any questions at all, just call.'

As he returned to the bed, Isobel pushed her empty plate away. 'Good news?'

'Yes. That was Clarissa, confirming she's still happy and it was good to talk last night.'

'What *was* all that about last night?'

He shook his head. 'It doesn't matter.'

'Yes, it does. Clearly it's important to you—and I'd genuinely like to know. I feel part of it now.'

'I'm planning on taking control of Cartwright's future. To do that I need the support of the minority board members, including Dillon and Clarissa.'

Isobel frowned. 'How does that work? Surely as a Cartwright you have enough clout to be able to do what you want.'

'It's more complicated than that.' He took a bite of his croissant.

'Go on.'

Seeing him hesitate, she felt a sudden stab of hurt. 'You can trust me.'

'I know that. I don't want to bore you.'

'You won't.' Swiftly, she put her plate on the floor and leant back against the headboard. 'Honestly.'

He shifted to sit beside her, leant back against the headboard and stretched his legs out against hers. 'Basically, my father owns forty-nine per cent of the shares, and I now own twenty per cent. The remaining thirty-one per cent is held by Dillon, Clarissa and two others. Until I was twenty-five my shares were held in trust and my father was able to use them to vote so he has been able to do whatever he wants to do.'

'And now you want to do things differently and your father doesn't agree.'

'Got it in one. When I first came into my shares at twenty-five, whatever I suggested he vetoed and the rest of the board agreed with him. But over the past four years I've won the board round, because they can see the validity of my ideas. I've also worked damned hard and they can't question my commitment any more.

I've put together a five-year plan and called a board meeting to vote on it.'

'Wouldn't it be easier to try and persuade your father that your ideas are good? Get his support?'

'That's not going to happen.'

'Why not?' Charles Cartwright didn't sound like an ideal parent, but surely he'd want his company to prosper.

'Because he's made it clear he doesn't want change, and he's not prepared to consider any of the proposals. That's his stand and he's told every one of the board members that. As far as I can tell, he wants to maintain the status quo; he thinks my plans are too risky and could affect his income and lifestyle. He also believes I won't have the staying power, that I'll give up at the first hint of trouble.' His body tensed next to hers. 'Forcing a vote is the only way I can do this, the only way to save Cartwright.'

'Have you spoken with him?'

'No.' He shrugged. 'There isn't any point. He doesn't do conversation with me.' His tone was flat. 'He never has.'

Isobel frowned, trying to connect all the events of his childhood. 'What happened after your grandfather took you in? Did you see your dad?'

'Occasionally, my grandfather took me to

visit him. But it never really worked. I ended up being looked after by one of my father's friends in another room and all I could hear was them yelling. I hated it. But then my grandfather died when I was six and I was devastated. I can remember the grief mixed with the sheer funk of not knowing what was going to happen to me.' Isobel reached out and interlaced her fingers through his; she knew that feeling all too well, the uncertainty and the fear of the future. 'But then someone turned up in a limo and drove me to my dad's. A huge mansion in London, full of bedrooms and people. I thought it was a party but after a while I realised that that's how my dad lives all the time.' He shook his head. 'I hardly ever saw him on his own. He was always with someone else.'

'Who looked after you?'

'Whoever was around. It was kind of a communal thing. Thankfully, he also employed an assistant, a kind of PA called Petra. She made sure there was always chilled champagne available and the right type of caviar and she also looked out for me, made sure I was fed, watered, clothed, enrolled at school.'

'But where was your father?'

'Sometimes he was around, sometimes he wasn't. There were times when he and his entourage would pack up and go to Nice for three months. Every so often he'd ruffle my hair, or ask me if I needed anything. One day when I was about eight, I told him yes, and I asked if I could go to boarding school. He shrugged and said, "Sure. Which one?" So that was that. After that I saw him occasionally; he'd always ask if I needed anything or tell me some anecdote about his latest conquest. That's it.'

'It doesn't sound like he spent a lot of time in the boardroom.'

'No. That's why I was surprised with how he reacted after I graduated. His refusal to give me a role at Cartwright.'

'And that's the first time he refused you anything?'

'Yup.'

'Which doesn't make sense. I still think you should talk to him. Ask him why.'

Jake sighed and her heart tugged at the sudden weariness in it. 'It wouldn't work, Iz. He and I don't work like that. In truth, we don't work at all. I've accepted that and moved on.'

Who was to say he was wrong? And yet it didn't make sense.

'It's just—' She hesitated and then decided to go on. 'There are so many things I wish I'd had the chance to talk to my mum about. So many unanswered questions, so many things, small and big. I didn't even have the chance to say goodbye.'

He shifted closer to her now, took her hand in his. 'What happened?'

'When I was ten I was taken into care.' The fact sounded so clinical. 'Teachers realised that my home life wasn't great. I'd become agitated at school, was bunking off and a teacher spotted the bruises. So I was taken into care. Entirely against my will, I might add. I kicked and screamed and they pretty much had to drag me out.'

He frowned. 'But…surely you wanted to get away.'

'I didn't want to leave Mum. I knew that, without me, everything would be so much worse for her. At least we had each other.' Guilt still rippled through her. 'I still wish I'd done things differently, hidden it better, figured out a way to stay with her.'

'But what about you? If you'd stayed—' He released her hand and put his arm around her instead, pulled her in close and safe, and she watched the emotions shadow his face.

'I know. And my head understands that social services had to step in. But I hated foster care—with all my heart. Being in care made me feel like a charity case, made me feel beholden, to the state and to the carers. As if I had moved out of Simon's power into the hands of social workers. Don't get me wrong, some of those people were good people—I know that. But, at the end of the day, to most carers I was a commodity, a job—a means of paying their bills. And when I became too much trouble they moved me on.'

Isobel gave a sudden smile and Jake studied her expression. 'I'm guessing you were a lot of trouble.'

'Yes, I was. My master plan was to be so bad I'd get sent back to Mum. Of course it didn't work out like that. All that happened was I ended up in a care home.'

'Where was your mum all this time? Did you see her?'

'Yes. But they were often supervised meetings or held in awful office buildings. I did try and sneak off and see her and we texted, but she didn't always turn up. Simon would stop her and I soon realised that her seeing me infuriated him, which meant he'd hurt her. So I stopped the visits, told her it was OK, that I'd got a plan. That as soon as I became sixteen I'd get a job, get myself together and I'd rescue her. Make her leave Simon and we'd live happily ever. That was my happy ever after dream.'

'What happened?' But she sensed he knew, just wanted to delay the inevitable conclusion.

'Ten days before my sixteenth birthday I found out my mum died of pneumonia.' The memory was a dark cloud of grief, disbelief. 'Due to an "administrative error" I only learnt of her death three months after it happened. She'd already been cremated. I wasn't even there. A friend, a woman I'd never heard of, sprinkled her ashes out to sea at Bournemouth. I don't even know why.'

Jake's arm was around her shoulders now, the weight the equivalent of a comfort blanket, and she turned to face him. His grey eyes were so full of concern. For her. The feeling was novel and wonderful, but she needed to get her point across.

'So you see I never got a chance to talk to her, I'll never know why Bournemouth; there are so many things I'll never know. So maybe, just maybe, you should think about talking to your dad.'

'I'll think about it. But first, I am so sorry for your loss.' His gaze was so full of sympathy, his focus entirely on her, and that sent a trickle of warmth through her; the sense that he genuinely cared made emotions swell and cascade inside her and she snuggled in even closer to the strength and comfort of his body. The sense of having shared these memories gave the moment an intimacy she'd never experienced before and it both moved and scared her. Enough that she shifted slightly away from him, needed to lighten the moment.

'Me too. But hey…' she smiled at him now '…it happened a long time ago and I've come to terms with it all. I just wish I could have said goodbye.' She shifted on the bed and looked at him again. 'Promise me you'll think about talking to your dad.'

He sighed. 'You don't give up.'

'Not easily.' A pause. 'So you promise?'

Now he chuckled and nodded. 'I promise.'

But sadness lingered in his eyes and she wanted to dispel it, wanted to clear memories of their parents from the room. 'Thank you. And then go for what you believe to be right.' She shifted to face him. 'But, in the meantime, I think *we've* talked enough.'

Now he smiled, the kind of smile that made her look down at her toes to see if they were actually curling in response.

'Sounds like you're looking for some action.'

'Action sounds like an excellent idea.'

'Got any suggestions?'

'Hmm. We could go for a run.' She kept her tone utterly serious and his expression fell in a ludicrous mix of puzzlement and disappointment and she couldn't keep it up.

She chuckled. 'Gotcha,' she crowed, and gave a squeal as he growled in mock anger.

'I have a way better idea than that.'

A few hours later Jake smiled across at Isobel; they were both seated in a local café tackling plates of lasagne and chips. God, she looked beautiful. Her hazel eyes were luminous, her skin glowed and warmth touched him at her closeness. The past hours had brought an intimacy he'd never experienced before, both physical and emotional—he'd shared experiences, opened up for the first time, and it felt both good and terrifying.

An alarm bell pealed in the back of his brain, warned him that he'd opened up and by definition that left him vulnerable. He shut it down, told himself that it was too late to worry, that maybe he and Isobel could figure something out—a way to stay connected, stay close. After all, Isobel wanted an independent relationship, one where she and her partner lived separate lives. Maybe that would work—maybe somehow he could manage to work every hour of the day and still see Isobel—maybe he'd think about this later.

Because there was something else he wanted to talk to Isobel about. 'I've had an idea.'

'Another one? Already?' She raised an eyebrow and he grinned.

'Not that sort of idea.' Now his expression sobered. 'And if you don't want to do it I won't be offended.'

'Go ahead.'

'I wondered if you'd like to go to Bournemouth. Maybe sit on the beach and you can say goodbye to your mum. We could take a balloon—' He stopped, realising how stupid that sounded. 'I did some research and apparently letting go of a balloon in memory of someone is a good way to say goodbye.' Still she said nothing and he shifted uncomfortably, wondering if he'd got this wrong. It was just that her story had touched him—her love and understanding for her mother, despite her mother's shortcomings, the weight of responsibility and guilt she carried. The tragedy of her childhood. All of it made him want to lighten her load. 'Sorry. This was a bad idea. I didn't mean to overstep, or intrude or try to understand your grief. I—'

'Stop.' Her voice was low and as she looked at him he thought he saw a tear gleam in her eye. 'It's a beautiful idea. Thank you and yes, I'd love to do that.'

And so a few hours later they arrived at

Bournemouth beach, Isobel clutching a helium-filled gold heart shaped balloon.

They sat down on the sand in a secluded spot and looked out at the waves, slightly choppy in the late afternoon breeze; clouds scudded across the sun, though the sand was still warm beneath them. She sat close to him, looking absurdly young and vulnerable as she stared out to sea.

'Mum loved gold things. I made her a picture once using a whole tube of gold glitter. I always hoped that one day I'd be able to buy her a real gold necklace. That's what makes death so sad—it takes away all those opportunities and dreams. When my dad died, my mum said what broke her heart most was all the things he'd miss.'

'What happened to your dad?' Isobel had never mentioned him, just that he'd died.

'He wanted to make a better life for his family, so he broke his own rules. He'd been made redundant, he was desperate so he took on a dodgy job, told my mum it was a one-off. It all went wrong and he ended up caught in a gang shoot-out. He died. I was still a baby so I have no memories of him at all, only a couple of photos. I used to think about him a lot, wonder what life would have been like if he hadn't made that one stupid choice. But, as you said, there is no point playing the what-if game. But it's tough not having any memories of someone.' She gave a small inhalation. 'I'm sorry, Jake. You know how that feels.' She shifted even closer to him. 'Have you seen your mum again since the first time?'

He shook his head. 'No. She's married with three kids, two boys and a girl. None of them know about me, even her husband doesn't, and she wants to keep it that way. I'll respect that.' Though he had thought about that long and hard—the idea that he had siblings out there who knew nothing about him and never would had imploded his world.

'That must be hard for you.'

'Yes.' He would always carry the sadness that his mother had stayed with them, brought them up, loved them but had walked away from him. Whatever the reasons. 'But it isn't something I can change. Perhaps one day she'll change her mind and tell them. Who knows?' He smiled at her. 'But this isn't about me. It's about you and your memories. You don't have any of your dad but you do remember your mum. Maybe the important thing is to remember the good times.'

'You're right. We used to love reading together. And we both loved ice cream. Mint choc chip. That was one of our favourite treats.

If it had been a bad day or a rough night, if we knew Simon would be out we'd sneak out to the park and sit on a bench with our ice creams. Sometimes we'd go on the swings and Mum would swing so high, as if she were trying to escape to freedom.'

'Hold that thought,' he said. 'We passed an ice cream van on our way down. I'll be back.'

He returned within minutes and handed her a cone and she smiled her thanks. 'I feel as though she is here, that somehow her spirit is watching. Does that sound daft?'

'No, it doesn't. I hope she can see you now, see how wonderfully you've turned out. I know she would be really proud of you—of everything you've achieved and the person you've become.'

'Even though I let her down? Failed to rescue her like I promised I would.'

'That wasn't your fault.' Somehow he needed to make her see that, believe it. 'You tried and she knew that. I'm sure that brought her happiness. You did everything you could to save her.'

'I know. I wish I could have saved her from herself, protected her from her own demons. But I couldn't. And sometimes she couldn't protect me. But the most important thing is that I know she loved me and I loved her.' Isobel looked up at the sky. 'Goodbye, Mum. I wish it could have been different. But I love you. I hope you knew that.'

Jake caught his breath as she let the balloon go, watched Isobel's face as she watched it drift upwards, saw the tears shine in her eyes and he tightened his arm around her, wished he could take the pain away.

They watched as the balloon floated upwards; caught by the breeze, it glittered in the sunlight as it bobbed and weaved its way. Buoyed by the wind, it dipped down and then up again, floated higher and higher until finally it was a tiny gold dot in the distance.

'Thank you.' She wiped away a tear and snuggled against him. 'Truly, thank you. That felt cleansing. As if I've made my peace. I will always wish her life could have been better, wish I could have had a happy ever after with her, but I know she did love me. And I can't change the past.' She shifted and she met his gaze. 'But if I could I would never have accused you six years ago. I should have known you are a good man.'

Happiness welled inside him and as she looked out to sea for the first time he did wonder whether if they had stayed together—could they, would they have made it? But, if they had, would he have still been on the verge of winning Cartwright?

The question chimed discord in his brain—the chips had fallen and now Cartwright was his priority. But, here and now, he wanted to simply enjoy this moment, this time with Isobel.

'How does a fish and chip dinner on the beach sound?'

'It sounds perfect.'

The next morning Isobel caught herself whistling as she cleared the breakfast dishes into the dishwasher, felt a hum of happiness in her veins as she tried to come up with a plan for the day. Perhaps they could laze the day away watching films and eating popcorn. The sheer cosiness of the idea made her smile. She clicked the dishwasher on and then looked round. Jake was in the lounge on a conference call to two of the board members.

Isobel glanced at the washing machine and decided she might as well put a wash on—the domesticity felt in keeping with her mood.

As she climbed the stairs and went over to the laundry basket, the idea of their clothes being mixed up seemed significant—ridiculously intimate—fuelling the growing part of her that couldn't help but wonder if maybe, just maybe, they could make this work. Yes, Jake was focused on work but so was she. Wouldn't it be better to see each other occasionally than never see each other again? It wouldn't be a 'short and sweet' contract, but perhaps they could negotiate different terms that suited them both. Or perhaps they could simply see what happened...

She pulled the washing out of the basket, automatically checked his jeans pockets for coins and her fingers found a twist of paper and she pulled it out, was about to put it on his side of the bed when she caught a glimpse of a scrawl of writing. A name she recognised. Before she could question the wisdom of it her fingers untwisted the paper and she read the words.

Hey, Tiger. Here you go! Call me.

This was followed by the digits of a mobile phone number.

Can't wait to have that fun!
Julia xxx

Isobel stared down at it. Read the words again. And again. She sank down onto the bed as the impact of the words crashed into her brain. Julia, Lucy's chief bridesmaid. Beautiful, svelte, blonde Julia. How could she have been such a fool? Julia even looked like bloody Anna; she'd known that.

Slow down, Isobel.

Jake had said, categorically said, he wasn't interested in her. And she'd believed him.

But if he wasn't interested why would he have her number? Why would she have felt it was OK to give him her number? Why had he even kept her number? Panic began to swirl inside her—panic that she'd got this oh, so very, very wrong.

She spun round as she heard the door open and saw Jake enter, a smile on his face—a smile that vanished when he saw her expression.

'Iz? What's wrong? What's happened?'

'This. This is what is wrong.' She couldn't even shout; all she could feel was an icy coldness inside her, as if her body was trying to protect her, ice her feelings.

'What is it?' He frowned and stepped forward as she handed him the paper. He read it and then looked at her, his eyebrows raised in query. 'I'm not getting this.'

'You can't see the problem?'

'No, I can't. I forgot I even had this.'

'You forgot you had a beautiful blonde's number in your pocket?' The high pitch of her voice echoed the shrill scream inside her, the tide of realisation that she'd been suckered.

'That is what I said, yes.' Now his voice had hardened slightly and her anxiety escalated and caused her skin to become clammy.

'OK. Well, now I've reminded you, perhaps you can tell me what it's doing in there.'

'Julia gave it to me at the wedding rehearsal.'

'Why?'

'You'd have to ask her. I assume it's because she wanted me to call her. I haven't even read it.'

'Then why did you take it?'

'What was I supposed to do?'

The question made her pause. Technically, at the wedding rehearsal Jake had been a free agent. But that wasn't the point. The point was that Jake had claimed not to be interested in Julia, had omitted to mention this note. He'd lied to her. She'd asked him time and again, given every opportunity for him to tell her, had even offered to further his cause. Yet all the time he'd kept Julia's number.

'You could have refused to take it. You could have told her you weren't interested. You could have thrown it away. So many options.'

'I didn't want to be rude to your problematic client's chief bridesmaid.'

'Then why did you keep it?'

'It would have been hurtful to chuck it away before her eyes and anyway there was a distinct lack of dustbins in the church. After that I forgot about it.' Anger sparked in his eyes. 'I'm not interested in Julia. We've been through this.'

A small part of her knew she had gone into fully fledged panic mode; she had to slow down, re-evaluate. Crossing her arms across her chest, she went to the window, her back to Jake whilst she tried to think, tried to impose some sort of order and logic despite the tornado of fear and hurt that swept through her. Fact: she'd suspected that Jake had an interest in Julia and vice versa. Fact: she'd asked Jake and he'd denied the interest. Fact: Jake had kept a note from Julia with her number. Conclusion: Jake could have lied.

Isobel closed her eyes in silent turmoil, opened them as she sensed Jake's approach. 'Isobel… Don't do this. There is nothing between Julia and me. You have to believe that.'

Oh, God. The mantra of *You have to believe me*, as espoused by Simon and her mother—and various foster carers. None of whom had been speaking the truth, however much she'd hoped they were.

But Jake wasn't Simon, wasn't any of those people and yet—how could she ignore the facts again? A second time. She'd decided to believe him about Anna, but now insidious doubts began to make tendrils into her brain, into her very heart. Had she been taken for a fool?

Had she believed what she wanted to believe? Been sidelined, distracted by his positive points—and there were many of those. Jake was nothing like her stepfather and she'd taken that to be enough. Jake was a good man—he'd helped Caro, would have protected Emily with his life, he'd shown Isobel care and support. But he was also a man who had told her himself that he kept his romances short and sweet, had no wish for commitment, a man who'd been brought up in an environment where fidelity was unimportant, lies a commonplace.

'I don't have to believe anything, Jake. For all I know, you were saving her details for your next short and sweet "romance". I suppose I should be pleased that this time you weren't going to sleep with her on my watch.'

She stood her ground as anger flared in his eyes and now she could almost hear the past echo into the room. The years spun backwards and they were back to that impasse again. The silence reverberated, rebounded, ricocheted around the room as they both absorbed her words—words she couldn't unsay even if she wanted to. And now she didn't know what she wanted, didn't know how it had come to this. From the joyous awakening that morning, the tangle of limbs, the kisses, the laughter, the safety of being cocooned in his arms—and now this.

This ugliness.

This reality.

He ran a hand over his face and she could see his attempt to contain anger, an anger that was palpable in the hardness of his jaw.

'I thought that chapter was closed. I thought you trusted me.'

'It was. I did. But now…' She faltered.

'Iz, I forgot I had the piece of paper in my pocket. I can barely remember what Julia looks like. I only took the damn thing out of politeness. It's the truth.'

So much of her wanted to agree, make this whole nightmare scenario go away, try to claw back to the happy day of watching films. But she couldn't. What if she was wrong, what if she was setting herself up again? As her mother had, again and again.

Yet Jake was nothing like Simon. *Could* this man who had taken her to Bournemouth to say goodbye to her mother, who had held Emily, stood up for Caro, taken her for cocktails, held her, listened to her, shared his own childhood with her, now be standing there lying to her?

Fact: yes, he could.

'You either trust me or you don't,' he said now. 'Your choice.'

'I want to,' she said softly.

'That's not enough.' The sadness in his eyes was palpable.

What to do? Twisting her hands together, she stared out of the window at the garden. Her choice. If you wanted to be with someone you believed in them. Only it didn't work like that, did it? If you *needed* to be with someone you conned yourself into believing them. When they lied to you, you deluded yourself, coated the words with glitter and gold to hide the ugly truth. You gave them power. You gave them control. She'd spent too long not in control, had known that Simon could do as he wished and she had no recourse or comeback. Same with social workers, foster carers. All she had known back then was that one day she and she alone would control her life. If you loved someone you became dependent on them, became weak, let them make a fool out of you. All because you were dependent on them.

Love.

This wasn't love—she wouldn't let it be.

Love was an illusory emotion that rendered you weak.

It was time to get out now, play it safe—maybe Jake was telling the truth, maybe he wasn't. The point was she didn't know, couldn't risk the latter. Or she'd be in too deep, on the verge, the edge of ceding control, handing over power.

'No, it's not enough,' she agreed.

The words tore at her heart and she could feel the hot prickle of tears threaten. This time there would be no comfort to be had from Jake, no arm round her shoulder, no kisses, no sympathy.

She stared at the cold, hard set of his face and waited for his reaction.

Jake felt rooted to the spot. The events of the past twenty minutes had come out of nowhere. A curve ball he'd not seen coming. How could he have stopped it? He didn't know, but he wished he could find a rewind button, wished he could see a way out of this.

But there wasn't one, not a gleam of light at the end of the midnight darkness of the metaphorical tunnel. Isobel didn't believe him. Again. She didn't believe him and there truly wasn't a damn thing he could do about that. Yet for a moment he wanted to try, to rant and rave. To yell and shout and make Isobel believe in him. Make her stay.

Dear God, would he never learn his lesson? You couldn't make people stay—he certainly

couldn't. The cold, hard pain of rejection solidified inside him and all his defence mecha-
nisms, learnt and honed over a lifetime, sprang
into place—took the pain, the hurt, the dull
ache of dismissal, the icy knowledge that she'd
judged him unworthy—and converted the
emotion into something he could use.

Aged eight, when he'd figured out nothing he could do would make his father notice
him, let alone love him, he'd taken that realisation—he'd used it, moulded it to take him
forward, figuring that boarding school was the
best route. At eighteen, when he'd realised his
mother still wanted nothing to do with him,
that his grandfather hadn't loved him, he'd
taken that, used it to fuel his ambition. All his
life he'd stood firm; Isobel had hurt him once
and he'd used that hurt and channelled it and
he could do it again.

He would use it to propel himself forward at
work, would use it to ensure he focused his en-
ergies where they should have been all along.
On Cartwright.

Yet as he looked at her, saw the pain on her
face, for one mad moment the urge to take her
into his arms persisted. But what could he say?
Isobel didn't trust him and she clearly never
would. This time was different—they'd both
shared so much and he'd believed that the bond

they had formed was stronger. Instead it had crumbled at the first test.

And still he oh, so nearly took that step forward. But he stopped himself. He wouldn't expose himself to that humiliation, that rejection—wishing for love that couldn't be given. He couldn't force love, couldn't force trust. He couldn't fight to win it, like knights of old. He knew that.

End of. It was time to roll with the punches, minimise the hurt and move on.

A repeat of six years ago, only this time the hurt was infinitely more; this time she *knew* him and had judged him. There could be no comeback from that.

'Then there is nothing more to say. Except goodbye.'

'Goodbye.' Her voice was a whisper as she turned and left the room.

How had he let this happen? Again.

Three days later

Isobel entered the park, looked round and saw Caro seated on a blanket, Emily by her side, surrounded by toys. She strode across the grass in a half run. 'So it's really true?'

'It's really true.' Caro's expression was a mix of relief and guilt. 'I feel absolutely awful for the poor man he assaulted but I'm so relieved that Martin is back behind bars and this time for a long time, I hope.'

'What happened?'

'The police turned up at the refuge to tell me. Martin got blind drunk and went on a tear. He smashed cars, windows, stole a car and then marched into Theo's offices. The security guard tried to stop him and Martin assaulted him. Badly. He was about to turn his rage on the receptionist when Theo got there.' Caro gave a small smile. 'It turns out Theo is a martial arts expert. He had Martin down in three minutes. He will also make sure the guard gets compensation. I went to visit him in hospital; he was so sweet. He said he'd rather Martin got him than me or the receptionist.'

'So you're free—' Isobel hugged her friend '—at least of Martin's presence.'

'Yes. It may take a while for the nightmares to stop. Or for me to trust anyone again.' Caro looked troubled.

'Theo?' Isobel guessed.

'Yes, I like him and I know he cares for me but I'm worried about so many things. Trusting him... Whether I can trust him, whether it would be foolish to rush in, whether if I ask him to wait I'll lose him, whether—'

'Take your time, Caro. It's early days yet. If he truly cares for you he will understand.'

'I know, and I also think that I need some time on my own, figuring what it's like to be independent, be just me...and Emily...without the fear of Martin overshadowing us. That's what I want—to live my life without fear. And if Theo sticks around, I'll give him a chance.' Caro tickled Emily's toes and then turned to her friend. 'But enough of me. What about you?'

'What about me?'

'You and Jake?'

'I told you. That ship has sailed.' It was a shame it had taken her broken heart with it. Because this time was so very much worse than the last time. This time she couldn't banish his image from her mind. Or her dreams.

Caro opened her mouth and then closed it again.

'What?'

'I just... It's hard to believe Jake lied like that. Again.'

I know that, she wanted to scream. Instead she shook her head. 'I will always be grateful to him for what he did for you and Emily, but I have to face the facts—I messed up.'

'You sure?'

Of course she wasn't sure. The doubts jumped and danced through her mind day and night, taunted her, urged her to call Jake. To give in. And she loathed herself for this dependency, this weakness, this need that she couldn't rid herself of. But she would.

'I'm sure enough,' she stated and leant forward to give Emily a kiss, avoiding the question in Caro's eyes.

Jake looked around his office and inhaled deeply. In an hour's time the board would convene. He'd present his proposal and put it to the vote and, barring any last-minute hitches, he'd win. This was what he wanted. This was more important than anything else. So why did he feel so—flat? The suspicion it was due to the constant ache of missing Isobel was an unwelcome one. But he did miss her, more than he would have believed possible. Her scent, her smile, her touch, the tickle of her hair, the way she snuggled into him.

Focus. On this meeting.

This was the meeting where he would bring his father down; he'd been working towards this goal for years—all his life. Jake frowned; discomfort edged his thoughts. Was that his goal—to vanquish his father? No. His aim was to do right by Cartwright, the company he loved and felt such a responsibility for. It was *nothing personal.*

Hell and damnation. Those were the words his mother had used and they sucked.

Now Isobel's voice echoed in his head. *'I still think you should talk to him.'*

An image of Isobel as she'd let go of the balloon, told her mother she loved her despite the things she'd done wrong. Her forgiveness, her understanding for her mother whilst accepting her flaws. The way Isobel had fought for Caro, even when Caro cut off contact with her.

'Promise me you'll think about talking to your dad.'

He'd promised he'd think about it, not actually do it. His father had paid a woman to have his baby, not because he wanted a child but because he didn't want to lose his lifestyle. His father had abandoned him as a tiny baby, let his grandfather have him.

But his father had at least chosen a woman who wanted the money for an altruistic reason, he had taken him in, he might not have shown him love but he had provided him with all material comforts, had agreed to his choice of school, of university—had denied him nothing. Except the thing he wanted most—a role in Cartwright. Why? Isobel was right—it didn't make sense.

Dammit.

Jake picked up the report and left the room, walked down to Charles Cartwright's lavish and largely unused office. Before he could change his mind, unsure even of what he meant to say, he knocked on the door.

'Come in.'

He entered and saw Charles' look of surprise. 'Jake.'

'Yes.' He approached the desk and Charles waved at the seat opposite. He sat, still wondered what to say.

After a while Charles cleared his throat. 'How can I help?'

'You can tell me why you are so opposed to this proposal.'

'Because I have no interest in growth. After I'm gone you can do what you like.'

'But why don't you have any interest in growth—in making the company more successful now?'

'I don't need a reason. I will vote against it.'

'Then why won't you give me a chance?'

'Why does that matter to you? You're going to try and take it, regardless of my reasons.'

There was little point in denial. 'Yes.'

Charles leant back and gave a mirthless laugh. 'You really are a chip off the old block. I'm sure your grandfather's spirit will attend the board meeting, will be there applauding you.'

His father's words brought a vivid image to mind and for a moment Jake could almost see Joseph Cartwright standing in the room, watching them with approval. Watching Jake, his coveted chosen heir, with approval as he tried to take Charles down. Suddenly the idea didn't sit well with him.

'This isn't personal. I'm doing this for Cartwright.'

Nothing personal. His mother's words. Again.

'Don't kid yourself. This is personal. Cartwright is personal. This company has dominated my life and it ruined my mother's. Your grandfather was obsessed with Cartwright and he was obsessed with the need for an heir. My mother was a kind, gentle, quiet woman and he treated her appallingly because she suffered miscarriage after miscarriage—until eventually they had me.'

Shame flushed Jake's face, heated his body with guilt—he'd never asked, never wondered about his grandmother, never questioned why the relationship between his grandfather and his father had gone wrong—had assumed the blame lay with his father.

'Surely that must have made him happy.'

'Nope. I was a perennial disappointment to him—a "namby-pamby mummy's boy", with no interest in his precious company or running it. I wanted to be an artist.' His bark of laughter was both self-derisory and mocking.

'Why didn't you?'

'Because if I had he would have thrown me out and I'd never have seen my mother again. So I decided to give up, to enjoy the money and the lifestyle and by the time my mother died I didn't want to give it up. I was enjoying myself too much.'

Yet Jake wondered now if he truly had.

'So when dear old Dad gave me the ultimatum about an heir I provided him with you—a worthy successor.'

Jake could hear the bitterness. 'But why didn't you look after me yourself?'

Now he saw genuine pain in his father's eyes. 'I miscalculated. When your grandfather gave me that ultimatum I should have decided to have a child in the right way, be a good father. But I was so consumed by my hatred of him, I decided to take him at his word, and so I turned you into a commodity. Then you were born; I took one look at you, so small, so vulnerable and I realised the enormity, the stupidity of what I'd done. I'd doomed you to a life without a mother and I panicked and then I did something I'll regret for the rest of my life. I ran, convinced myself that was for the best. I left Petra to arrange a nanny; I knew my dad would come to claim his own soon enough. I told myself you'd be better off with him. I left because I was too weak to fight for you, because the battle was over before it began. I had nothing to give you. That decision has haunted me ever since.'

The anguish in his father's eyes was genuine and Jake could sense, could feel his emotion. Yet he still didn't understand. 'But when he died why didn't you try to bond with me then?'

'It was too late and I didn't know how. Plus, how could you ever forgive me for what I had done? I couldn't expect that of you. I did what I could, gave you whatever you wanted.'

'Except Cartwright.'

Charles nodded. 'I wanted to allow you to go your own way, not to have to tie yourself to Cartwright. I want you to have the chance to have a different life, be what you want to be. Not be consumed by Cartwright like your grandfather was.'

Jake hesitated. Was he consumed?

His dad continued. 'I've watched you the past four years and all you have done has been focus on Cartwright. Everything. Tell me what is the most important thing in your life.'

The answer was automatic. 'Isobel.'

For a long moment father and son stared at

each other and then, for the first time, Charles smiled, a genuine smile. 'Then there is hope for you yet.'

Isobel opened the door of the flat and blinked. 'Roberto?' Not that there was a need for the question. It was definitely Jake's driver.

The man smiled at her. 'Jake asked me to deliver this.'

Isobel looked down at the invitation, complete with embossed writing.

> *Mr Jake Cartwright*
> *invites*
> *Ms Isobel Brennan*
> *to a meeting at*
> *Cartwright of Mayfair*
> *at 8:00 p.m. on Friday*

She looked at her watch. 'It's nearly 6:00 p.m. now,' she pointed out.

'Yes. If you agree to attend the meeting, I can take you straight there.'

'But…' Isobel looked down at her clothes— on the plus side she wasn't in her pyjamas. On the down side her jeans and oversized checked flannel shirt weren't a whole load better.

'What to do? What to do?' Oh, God. She'd said the words out loud.

Roberto cleared his throat. 'Um… I know it's not my place but we—that's Maria, Stefan and me—we think you should come and see him. He's—'

'He's what?'

'He hasn't been himself since the two of you…since…you left. I'm not trying to force you to do anything. But Jake is a good man.'

Isobel sighed, knowing she couldn't send Roberto on his way. In truth, she was relieved for the excuse to go—she would go for Roberto, for Stefan, for Maria. Not because her whole being craved the sight of Jake.

'Let's go,' she said. If Jake wanted to meet her at Cartwright he'd have to accept her as she was. It occurred to her suddenly that he always had. It had been Isobel who worried and agonised over whether she would fit. He'd never cared. Not six years ago and not ten days ago.

The drive passed in easy conversation and she was grateful to Roberto for initiating simple topics; she learnt about his family, that he was in fact Maria's son-in-law, how much he enjoyed his job, his love of cars.

Once they approached Cartwright he smiled and dropped her at the entrance. 'Good luck.'

Her heart pounded against her ribcage and she considered turning around and running as fast as her trainers could carry her. Knowing that would be the coward's way out, instead she stepped through the revolving door and into the marbled lobby, looked around and there he was.

Jake.

Isobel halted, tamed the urge to move closer to him. Bad enough she now knew how a parched plant must feel when the first raindrops scattered down in nourishment. But she couldn't help the need to look, to absorb his image—the warm strength of him, the spikiness of his blond hair, the set of his jaw, the mesmerising grey eyes. An image she put onto the lock screen of her brain.

It occurred to her that as she'd stood rooted to the spot he too had been looking at her and she wondered what thoughts crossed his mind. He stepped forward. 'Thank you for coming. I wasn't sure if you would. Come through.'

Belatedly, it occurred to her that the lobby should have been busier on a Friday night. She shrugged the knowledge off as unimportant as they walked down the richly carpeted corridor, followed discreet signage to the hotel's signature restaurant.

Great. He was taking her to dinner in a Michelin-starred restaurant full of rich designer-clad people and she was in her Cowboys 'r' Us outfit. Well, tough—if he was trying to prove a point, whatever that was, so be it. She'd walk in and be herself.

But as he pushed the door to the restaurant open she frowned, her senses on alert. Something was off, missing, not how it should be. Then she realised—there was no hum of chatter, no clatter of knives and forks, none of the noises you'd associate with a busy restaurant on a Friday evening.

As she entered it became clear why. The room was empty, dimly lit, apart from a table in the centre. As she stepped closer she gave a small gasp of appreciation. An array of candles flickered and dappled the flower-strewn surface. Snowy white linen napkins, silver cutlery, crystal glasses.

And as Jake held out her chair, piano music filled the air. Isobel looked across the room to where the grand piano stood in its glory, recognised the same pianist they had listened to in Oxford.

She looked around the room. 'What's going on?' she asked.

'We're having dinner. I figured you'd prefer it without an audience. The pianist can't hear us.'

'You've closed the restaurant? What about all the guests?'

'They have been suitably compensated. No

one is missing out; I've made sure of that.' Before he could say any more a waiter appeared and placed two plates in front of them.

Isobel looked down at a beautifully presented dish of scallops, with crispy pancetta, complete with a circle of butter flecked with green and slices of— 'Apple?' she asked.

'Pickled apple,' Jake said.

'And what have you got?'

'Lemon sole with samphire and bacon and sweet potato fries. I thought we could go halves.'

Isobel took a deep breath. 'Jake, the food is lovely, the table is lovely, but what the hell is going on?' It was a question she could well ask herself. This man had lied to her, splintered her heart, yet she was here.

'I thought we should try and get closure now, rather than wait six years and hope fate gives us another shot. I don't want a repeat of six years ago, where you decide I'm a lying bastard, I defend myself, you walk out and I let you go.'

'Which bit do you want to change?'

'Pretty much all of it. But, most of all, the bit where you leave. Six years ago I didn't fight. I figured you can't make people love you, you can't make them stay, just like I couldn't make my mother or my father love me. Or stay. That's still true. You can't force someone to love you. But there is something I can do. I can't force you to love me but I can tell you the truth. That I love you.'

Her fork clattered into the scallops, tumbled onto the linen tablecloth. He loved her?

Isobel sat frozen, her whole body in shock, her brain in conflict. Every instinct informed her that Jake was genuine, but all she could do was listen.

'Six years ago I was too hurt and angry and scared to say it. I'm still hurt and angry and, yes, I'm still scared but this time I want you to know you are loved.'

Isobel stared at him, opened her mouth to shout that she loved him back. But something stopped her.

What was it? Then realisation crashed in on her. It was fear. What had Caro said to her? That she didn't want to live her life with the fear of Martin overshadowing her. Wasn't that what Isobel was doing—still living in fear? Fear of a relationship, fear of sharing, fear of letting love into her life.

The knowledge was absolute and tears prickled the back of her eyelids in a bid to escape and she heard Jake's curse.

'Iz? I didn't mean to make you cry. I won't say another word. I wasn't trying to put pressure on you. I—'

She summoned a smile, swiped her eyes with the back of her hand. 'Stop. It's OK. I love you too.' The words liberated her as the shadow of fear receded. 'I love you,' she repeated. 'I've just been too scared to admit it.' She'd been caught in Simon's thrall of fear: fear of love or trust. 'Scared to let it in. Because I thought love bred fear, equalled weakness and gave power. But it doesn't.' It all seemed so much clearer now, as if lit up by the light of real love. Because the bond between her mum and Simon hadn't been love—it was a travesty of love. The knowledge seemed so obvious now, but it hadn't been. It had taken Jake's love and understanding and his actions over the past week to make her see it.

She came to a stop. Saw the shell-shocked look in Jake's grey eyes.

'You love me?' There was a whisper of disbelief in his voice and that hint of vulnerability from this strong man tore her heart as she realised that she might be the first person to say the words to him in his life.

'Yes, I love you.' She took his hand in hers, wanting, needing a physical connection. 'I loved you six years ago but I needed to believe Anna, because the alternative was to trust you, trust myself. A week ago I still couldn't take that leap—it was still easier to walk away than to trust you. I'm sorry I doubted you, when I know you are honourable and good and truthful.

'I love you for your strength and your understanding and your capacity to listen. You have never tried to browbeat me or make me agree with you. You have listened, really heard me. And you have accepted me—who I am, whether it's in a designer dress or jeans and a T-shirt. You took me to Bournemouth and a glamorous ball. You've made me realise that you can love someone and you can rely on them but that doesn't make you needy or dependent. I can still strive to be the best at what I do with you by my side.'

Now Jake's smile had hit beam status as he raised a hand. 'My turn. I love you because you're caring, kind, loyal, fierce in your determination, so courageous to have overcome everything you had to face in your childhood. Yet you have come out a good, beautiful person who can see the good in people. You made me see that there are things and people that are worth fighting for. That there is more to life than work. Thanks to you, I spoke to my dad.

'And I get being scared. I was too scared of being abandoned, rejected again. When you left six years ago it hurt. So very much…but I couldn't fight because I thought there was no point. I thought it would intensify the pain to try and fail. But now I know that the risk is worth it—that there was every reason, even if I only got the chance to tell you I love you.' His arm tightened around her. 'But I much prefer this ending,' he said. 'The one where we love each other. For ever,' he added firmly. 'I know there are no guarantees but I'm damn sure this is a lifetime partnership. Of two equals.'

'Yes.' Her voice was serious now. 'That's something else you've shown me. It doesn't matter how much money you have or what your background is. You and I work. As a team. We fit.' The concept brought a smile to her face. And then the meaning of his words sank in. 'You talked to your dad? What happened?'

He exhaled a small sigh and she squeezed his hand gently. 'It turns out that it's more complicated than I thought. He's not the terrible person I thought he was.' As she listened to what had taken place, hope surged in her heart that maybe something could be salvaged, some sort of relationship be forged.

'So what happened at the meeting?'

'I withdrew my proposal. I explained that I would prefer to get it through with my father's support, if at all possible. And my father and I— we've decided to talk. If I can show him this is truly what I want I think he'll give me his backing, but I understand that for him Cartwright is a monster, whereas for me it's something beautiful. But, whatever happens, I will not get consumed—you will always be more important. And if we have children so will they.'

'Children?'

'Only as and when we both agree it's right. But, yes, I would love to have children with you. Not hypothetical ones but real ones. Because I don't believe we will repeat our parents' patterns—I know you will be an amazing mum.'

'And I know you will be an amazing dad.' That belief was heartfelt. Jake had been abandoned, treated with a confusing indifference and yet his inherent goodness, his honour and his principles shone through in all his actions. And he would give his child all the love and attention he had been starved of. Just as she would ensure her child was safe, secure and loved and she would always put her child first. There was no reason to fear the repeat of a pattern, no reason to live in the shadow of fear any more.

'And I know our children are going to be incredibly amazing,' Jake said. 'But not until you're ready. I know how important your work is to you as well and I respect that.'

Isobel nodded—the idea of a family, of having children with this man swelled her heart with love and joy.

Jake gestured to the plates. 'But in the meantime I think it's time for dessert.'

Isobel nodded, her head spinning, giddy with joy, and a few minutes later she smiled up at the waiter as he placed a plate in front of her. 'It's beautiful,' she exclaimed.

The waiter gave a small bow. 'Enjoy,' he said and left, just as the pianist struck up a gorgeous blues song; the notes strummed the air evocatively, seemed to complement the happiness that bubbled inside her.

She studied the spun sugar confection, a beautiful delicate cage that topped a golden egg. Carefully she removed it.

'Allow me,' Jake said and he rose, moved to her side and unscrewed the egg.

Isobel eyes widened and she gave the smallest of gasps. Inside were beautiful colourful sugar roses, pink, red, and white, each one exquisite in its detail. And nestled amongst them was a ring—a classic single solitaire diamond glittered and glinted in the candlelight.

Jake reached in and took it out and dropped to one knee.

'Isobel, will you marry me? So that we can walk together through life. I promise I will be there for you through good times and bad, I want to hold you and love you and be by your side for the rest of my days.' Now he gave the smallest and wickedest of smiles. 'And nights. You are my life, my soul, my love, my balance.'

Tears of joy tickled the back of her eyes as she rose and pulled him to his feet. 'I will marry you—I want to spend my life with you. You have my full trust and I give you my love without reserve or condition for ever.'

And as he slipped the ring onto her finger she knew that she had found the one place she would always fit, would always be loved for herself and would always be safe.

* * * * *

*If you enjoyed this story,
check out these other great reads from
Nina Milne*

Their Christmas Royal Wedding
Whisked Away by Her Millionaire Boss
Hired Girlfriend, Pregnant Fiancée?
Conveniently Wed to the Prince

All available now!